Berkley Street

Written by Ron Ripley
Edited by Emma Salam and Lance Piao

ISBN-13: 978-1532759208
ISBN-10: 1532759207
Copyright © 2016 by ScareStreet.com

Thank You and Bonus Novel!

I'd like to take a moment to thank you for your ongoing support. You make this all possible! To really show you my appreciation for purchasing this book, I've included a bonus scene at the end of this book. **I'd also love to send you the full length novel: Sherman's Library Trilogy in 3 formats (MOBI, EPUB and PDF) absolutely free!**

Download Sherman's Library Trilogy in 3 formats, get FREE short stories, and receive future discounts by visiting www.ScareStreet.com/RonRipley

Keeping it spooky,
Ron Ripley

Chapter 1: Shane, September 1st, 1982

Shane Ryan had never seen a bigger house.

Their new home looked like a castle, with two towers and tall, narrow windows. Shane counted six chimneys. A pair of giant, thick trees stood on either side of the wide front door. A thick stone wall, nearly as tall as Shane's father, protected the whole property.

"What do you think, kid?" his father asked as he parked the car in the long driveway.

"Is it a castle?" Shane asked.

His mother let out a pleased laugh, and his father shook his head.

"No, kid. The Andersons, well, they were really wealthy. They wanted it to look like a castle on the outside, but on the inside, well, it's a regular house."

"Oh," Shane said, trying not to sound disappointed. "So no secret passages or anything?"

"Who knows?" his mother said, gently slapping his father on the arm. "Who knows?"

"Yeah," Shane's father said, winking at him in the rearview mirror, "Who knows?"

"Come on," Shane's mother said. "Let's go inside."

His father turned the engine off, and Shane dutifully waited for his mother to open the back door of the Cadillac before he got out. The September air was warm and still smelled like summer. Shane saw the grass in the yard was freshly mowed and all of the windows shined. Each gray stone seemed to glow in the sun.

"How big is the yard?" Shane asked, looking around.

"Well," his father said, following his son's gaze, "you could fit eight of our old yards into the front yard."

"Wow," Shane said, turning and looking at the expanse of grass.

"In the side yard there's a garden," his mother said, "there's also a pond in the backyard."

Shane felt his eyes widen. "A pond?"

"Yup," his father said happily. "And you know what else, kid?"

"What?" Shane asked.

"It's full of fish. We can go fishing whenever we want."

"Wow," Shane whispered. "Wow."

Shane's parents laughed happily, and he followed them up the front walk. His father took out the house key, unlocked the large door and opened it. Shane stepped into the biggest room he had ever seen.

A huge set of stairs stretched up into darkness, and dim pieces of furniture filled what he realized was a hallway. Close to where Shane stood, a tall grandfather clock ticked away the time.

And behind the tick of the second hand, Shane heard whispers.

Someone whispered in the walls.

Chapter 2: Shane, March 20th, 2016

The fan hummed steadily.

Shane sat up in his narrow bed as the cool air dried the sweat on his body. He took long, deep breaths and looked at the clock.

Six in the morning.

He closed his eyes and forced away the last remnants of his nightmares. He reached over to his bed table, took the bottle of whiskey and glass off of it and poured himself a small shot.

Shane drank it quickly and returned them both to their place.

My security blanket, he thought bitterly. He got out of the bed, took the three steps to his bathroom and climbed into the shower. Shane turned on the water and forced himself to stand under it until it warmed up. Finally, with the water tolerable, he scrubbed himself rigorously and then rinsed off.

The bare minimum to get clean and rid himself of the stench of fear and sweat.

Once out of the shower, he dried off and looked at himself in the mirror.

Thin face. Haggard eyes. No hair.

Alopecia areata, he thought, running a hand over his smooth scalp. His pale skin looked sickly in the light of the fluorescent lamp above the mirror. *Unexplained hair loss.*

Pretty sure I can explain it, Shane thought angrily.

With a shake of his head, he forced himself to focus on his morning routine. He brushed his teeth, went back into his bedroom and got dressed. A pair of jeans and a black tee shirt. Running shoes and a pullover sweatshirt of dark gray. Absently he rolled the wedding band on his ring finger as he walked to his kitchenette.

Oatmeal for breakfast. Strong coffee. Vitamins. A banana and two pieces of rye bread toasted.

No matter how much he ate, though, he wouldn't get up over one hundred and forty-five pounds.

Tall and thin, he thought. *Just like dad.*

Shane put his wallet in his pocket, took his phone and his keys, and left his apartment. The noises of the world fell in around him, and he did his best to ignore them. He took his walk alone in the early morning light. The streets were clear of snow, although salt and sand crunched beneath his feet.

Winter had slipped by New Hampshire and snow had been a rare sight. Ice, however, had visited more than once, and the streets were always treated for it.

Shane fought the urge to stop at the Paki's corner store for a pack of cigarettes, but he walked by. He reached the top of Library Hill, walked around the Soldiers and Sailors Monument, and made his way back to his apartment on Locust Street.

Once inside, he poured himself a fresh cup of coffee and went to his laptop. He powered it up, logged into his work account, and looked to see what needed to be translated.

Among the work emails, he found one from O'Connor Law Associates.

Oh, Jesus, what now? He thought, opening the email.

His heart leaped at what it said.

Dear Mr. Ryan, the email began. *We are pleased to inform you the proceedings regarding your family's home at 125 Berkley Street have finally finished. The house is yours, per your parents' wishes, and your uncle and aunt have exhausted their financial and legal options. Please call my office at your earliest convenience so we might sign the appropriate paperwork and give you the keys to your home.*

Sincerely,

Jeremy O'Connor.

Shane sat back and stared at the email.

The keys to my home.

My home.

Shane leaned forward and jotted the number for the firm down on his notepad.

Now I'll find them, he told himself, joy and rage twining together in his heart. *Now I will find them.*

Chapter 3: Shane, September 15th, 1982

"Are you awake?"

Shane sat up and turned on his light. His heart beat quickly, and he looked around his large room. The curtains were drawn on the tall windows. His books were lined neatly on his shelves. Legos were scattered across the floor by the old fireplace.

"Are you awake?" the voice asked again.

Shane twisted around in his bed. Neither his mother nor his father was in his room.

He was alone.

He couldn't tell where the voice came from. His mouth was dry, so he swallowed, wet his lips with his tongue, and said in a low voice, "I'm awake."

"Good," the voice said.

It came from behind his dresser.

"Why? Why is it good?" Shane asked.

"Because they don't want you here," the voice said. "They don't want you. Here."

His heart thumped heavily, and he managed to ask, "Who?"

"Don't ask," the voice said. "I want you here. I'm lonely."

Shane tried to speak but couldn't. The sound of his blood as it rushed through him nearly drowned out his own thoughts. "Why are you lonely?" Shane whispered.

"I've been here a long time. Such a very long time."

The bureau started to move, inch by inch, into the room. It swung out slowly from the wall, and a dark shadow appeared.

It took Shane a moment to realize there was a passage in the wall.

A soft scrape slipped out of the darkness, and it was quickly followed by a sigh.

The speaker stepped into the room.

A girl. Perhaps eight or nine.

And dead.

Dead, dead, dead.

She smelled like death, and her skin was shrunken, pulled tight across her bones. Her lips were stretched in a gruesome smile, and long teeth protruded from her yellow jawbone.

"I'm lonely," she said, stepping into the room. Bits of fabric fell from her ragged, gray dress. Her brown hair was tied back with a faded red bow, and the bones of her feet cracked as she walked. "I'm lonely. I want to play."

Shane closed his eyes, opened his mouth, and screamed.

Suddenly his bedroom door was thrown open and bounced against the wall, and Shane opened his eyes. His father and mother charged into the room, their faces puffy with sleep and their hair disheveled.

"Oh my God, Hank," his mother said, pointing to the bureau.

"What the hell?" his father asked. His father walked to the bureau as his mother hurried to Shane.

Shane sank into his mother's arms and shook as she held him tightly. From the protection of his mother's embrace, Shane watched his father.

"There's a passage," his father said, looking back at Shane and his mother. "Fiona, there's a passage here."

"What?" she asked. "Are you sure?"

"Positive. Looks like we put his bureau against a door of some sort. Couldn't even tell. You'd think it was part of the wainscoting. Hell, I did."

Shane's father leaned into the dark hole the dead girl had come from.

His father backed out and looked at his mother. "It's a real passage, Fiona. I can't see much in there right now, but I thought I saw lights. It's just wide enough for someone to walk through."

"Servants' passage?" she asked.

"Must be," he answered.

Shane watched as his father pushed the bureau back into place.

"It wasn't in any of the forms, Hank," Shane's mother said. "There wasn't anything about servants' passages. Just their quarters."

"Yeah," his father said. "I know."

7

Shane's shakes slowly went away, and his father came and sat down on the bed beside him.

"Did you get scared, kid?" his father asked.

Shane nodded.

"Would have scared me too," his father said.

"There was a girl," Shane whispered.

"What?" his mother asked.

"A girl. A dead girl," Shane said.

"Shane," his father started, and Shane heard the 'now you're seven, so you need to be a big boy' voice, but his mother interrupted him.

"Hank," she said, her voice harsh. "Not now."

"Okay, Fiona. Okay," his father said with a sigh.

"Is there a way you can block the bureau so it won't pop open again?" his mother asked.

"I'll figure it out," Shane's father said, nodding.

"Good. Shane," his mother said. "Do you want me to lie down with you for a bit?"

Shane clung to his mother and nodded.

Chapter 4: Standing in Front of Hell

Shane smoked steadily as he leaned against an old oak tree and looked at his house.

His monstrous familial home.

His hand shook as he tugged the cigarette out of his mouth and exhaled.

The keys he had picked up from the attorney sat heavily in his pocket. Shane wanted to go through the gate. He wanted to walk up the driveway and unlock the front door. It was his right, and his responsibility to enter the home. He sighed and took another drag from the cigarette.

An older man walked towards him from the dead portion of Berkley Street. He had an older German shepherd on a short leash; the dog's brown and black fur glistened in the mid-morning light.

The older man frowned as he looked at Shane, and Shane knew what the old man saw; a middle-aged man who leaned against a tree and smoked a cigarette. A man who stared at a house empty for decades.

Shane looked, he knew, like a criminal.

The older man, whose skin was pale, and his hair gone, adjusted his grip on the dog's leash and paused half a dozen feet away from Shane.

"Hello," the old man said, and Shane heard the authority and command in his voice.

He's used to being obeyed, Shane thought. He fought the desire to make the conversation difficult for the old man.

"Hello," Shane said simply. He finished his cigarette, stubbed it out and held onto the butt. Once he was sure the embers were out he slipped the remains of the tobacco into his pocket.

The stranger looked at him curiously.

"Do you always police up your cigarettes?" he asked.

"Yes," Shane nodded. "Ever since I saw a drill instructor crawl up one side and down the other of a kid who tossed his butt onto the ground."

The old man chuckled.

"I quit a long time ago," the stranger said. "But I experienced something similar."

"Nice weather for a walk," Shane said, conversationally. He wondered when the man would get to the point.

"Do you live around here?" the old man asked, politely but pointedly.

Shane nodded.

"Do you mind if I ask where?" the stranger said.

Shane looked at the man. He could see the stamp of the Marine Corps on him. The man's back was ramrod straight, his eyes steady. He was probably in his seventies, but Shane suspected the man could still hold his own in a fight.

"I don't mind at all. I live there," Shane said, nodding towards his house.

The stranger frowned, confused. "No one lives there, son."

"I do. Now. I lived there before too. A long time ago, though," Shane said.

The man's eyes widened slightly. "Are you the Ryans' boy?"

"I am," Shane said. Impulsively he offered his hand and introduced himself. "Shane Ryan."

The stranger shook it. "Gerald Beck."

"A pleasure," Ryan said.

"This is Turk," Gerald said, patting the top of his dog's head. "He and I are both retired."

"Police dog?" Shane asked.

"No," Gerald said, shaking his head. "Just an old dog. He came from a shelter up in Enfield. He's a little jumpy sometimes. I try not to walk him by your house too much. Tends to upset him."

"But you saw me loitering?" Shane asked, grinning.

Gerald chuckled and nodded. "Yes. I did. I'm a nosy old maid sometimes."

"No problem with it," Shane said. He looked back at the house. The windows seemed to look back at him. A shiver danced along his spine and Shane returned his attention to Gerald. "So, you're a Marine?"

"Yes," Gerald said proudly. "Infantry. Korea and Vietnam. First Marine Division. You?"

"Forward observer, America's Battalion," Shane said. "Did a couple of tours in Afghanistan. One in Iraq."

Gerald looked at him for a minute. "Fallujah?"

Shane nodded.

"We had heard you joined the military. I wasn't close to your parents, so I didn't know what branch," Gerald said apologetically.

Shane smiled at the man.

"I heard there was some difficulty with the house in regards to ownership," Gerald said.

"It's cleared up now," Shane said.

"You thinking about whether or not to go in?" Gerald asked.

"Yeah," Shane said softly. Then with more determination, he said, "Yes."

"Well," Gerald said, "when you're done, you're welcome to come down and say hello. I live up the road at one sixty-six. Just ring the bell. I've always got coffee on. It's just me and Turk in the house."

"I will," Shane said. "Thank you."

"You're welcome, son," Gerald said. He started to walk away, and Turk followed him. Gerald glanced over his shoulder and called back, "Anytime."

Shane raised a hand and nodded with a smile. He waited a few minutes after the older man, and the dog had left before he straightened up. Shane focused on the front door and started to walk towards it.

Chapter 5: Graduation, Parris Island, South Carolina, 1994

Shane sat with Corey's family. He smiled at Corey's mom, who was fawning over her son, and looked out over the parade ground for his parents. They had promised they would make his graduation from boot camp. They had even reserved rooms on Parris Island.

Shane felt proud; he had earned the title of United States Marine, and it was Family Day. He wanted his family there.

Where are they? He asked himself, peering through the crowd of people.

He couldn't see them.

Drill Instructor Allen came from around a group surrounding Davidson and made his way to Drill Instructor Carter, who stood off to one side and chatted with Ramirez. Allen leaned in close, said something to Carter, and the two Drill Instructors turned and looked at Shane.

Shane stiffened.

It didn't matter if he had just graduated, those men were still NCOs, and they could make life hell until he shipped out.

A wave of nervous fear ripped through him as they walked closer.

"Private Ryan," Carter said.

"Aye, sir," Shane said, standing up quickly. Out of the corner of his eye, he saw Corey tense.

"Come with us, Private," Carter said.

"Aye, sir," Shane said. He quickly followed the two Drill Instructors to a distance away from the rest of the class, to where the chaplain stood alone, a look of concern on his face.

"Private Ryan," the chaplain said. "We've received some news about your parents."

"Sir?" Shane asked.

"Your parents are missing, Private Ryan," the chaplain said.

Shane blinked and shook his head. "What are you saying, sir? Missing? On the road somewhere?"

"From your house," the chaplain said in a gentle voice. "They've vanished."

Shane closed his eyes and shook his head.

The house, Shane thought numbly. *It took them.*

He suddenly felt hands under his arms. They gripped his biceps firmly and applied just enough pressure to support him. Although he wanted to drop to his knees, Shane found he couldn't.

"Easy, Ryan," Drill Instructor Allen said in a soothing tone. "Easy. It's alright."

"How long?" Shane managed to ask.

"At least a week," the chaplain said. "Your parents were just gone, though. From what I was told, everything is there. Their wallets, money. The car. The police aren't sure what happened."

Shane tried to stand on his own but his legs wouldn't obey.

Drill Instructor Carter leaned in to help.

"You're okay, Marine," Carter said. "You're going to be okay."

Shane knew he would be, but it didn't make the vanishing of his parents any easier.

Chapter 6: Finding Courage

It took Shane another ten minutes to build up the courage to even cross the sidewalk and step onto his property.

His uncle and aunt had fought him since his parents had initially disappeared. They had even hinted at Shane's possible involvement in their vanishing.

The courts, of course, had found it to be a baseless accusation. The United States Marine Corps could confirm he had been present at the Recruit Training Depot at Parris Island, South Carolina, the entire time.

Shane had never liked his Uncle Rick or his Aunt Rita. At one point he had even hated them after the court cases had begun. He didn't any longer, though. They weren't worth his time or effort. He had allowed his lawyers to handle the case, and they had.

The house was his.

The house was *his*.

If a house like this can belong to anyone, Shane thought.

With a grimace, he squared his shoulders and stepped across the sidewalk to the asphalt of the driveway and started the long walk to the front door. Shapes flicked in and out of the various windows. He told himself to ignore the shadows of birds and clouds.

But he knew neither of those had reflected in the old glass.

Nothing ever reflected in the old glass.

Even the sun was defeated by the house.

Shane felt the urge to spit but found his mouth to be dry. He kept his breath steady and approached the house carefully.

The keys shook in his hands as he took them out of his pocket and stepped up to the front door.

He slid the key in, heard the lock tumble, and he twisted the doorknob.

It opened easily, as though it had been only yesterday when he had last been inside, instead of the day he had left for boot camp.

A soft breeze rolled over him and carried with it the scent of lilacs. His mother had hated lilacs and despised how the house was never quite free of the smell. The house was cold as he stepped in.

And the door closed quickly behind him of its own accord.

Shane managed not to jump.

I need to get the power turned back on, he thought, looking around. Sunlight filtered in through the tall, narrow windows, but Shane knew he needed electricity. And water and sewerage, and all of those other things. Someone had suggested he contact a plumber, in case the pipes had burst over all the cold New England winters, but Shane knew he didn't need to worry about it.

Nothing would happen to the house.

He looked around and saw the furniture still placed exactly as he remembered it. Everything was absent of dust, as though someone had cleaned the home just for him.

And they probably have, Shane thought with a sigh.

He walked slowly through the first floor. He passed into and out of the parlor, the dining room, the living room, the game room, and the butler's pantry. He ignored the second floor and the basement. He needed more sunlight, and more courage than he had at the moment.

He stood in the kitchen and looked out the back door. A wide porch swept out towards the backyard and the pond. Behind him, he heard whispers, low voices.

He couldn't understand any of what they said, but he knew it wasn't pleasant.

He had heard it all before.

Long before his parents had vanished.

He focused his attention on the pond. What little light was left in the day seemed to be swallowed by the water.

Shane stiffened, focused on the center of the pond and stared.

Just beneath the water, he saw it. A strange white shape which twisted and undulated. Shane caught sight of hair and the glitter of eyes.

She watched him.

She remained.

Shane turned to the counter, went to the sink and threw up the coffee and protein bar which had served as lunch. He spat several times into the sink to rid his mouth of the taste.

Suddenly the pipes clanked under the cabinet, and he took a nervous step back.

"The water's on, Shane," a voice whispered from behind him.

He snapped around but saw nothing.

The faucet groaned, and water splashed loudly into the sink.

With a shudder, he turned around and saw the water. It came out of the tap quickly. After a moment of shock Shane took a step forward, pulled up the sleeves on his sweatshirt, and started to rinse the vomit down the drain.

Something cold brushed his ear and an old voice hissed, "Welcome home, Shane."

Shane did his best to ignore it and focused instead upon the wretched, acidic smell of his own bile.

It was better by far.

Chapter 7: Shane, May 3rd, 1983

Shane was ready.

In three more days he would be eight years old. He wasn't going to be scared anymore.

He wasn't going to have to sleep with the light on anymore, or with the bedroom door taken off the hinges

Shane wasn't going to be afraid anymore.

The grandfather clock downstairs in the main hallway struck midnight and Shane waited. After the last chime, he heard someone scratch behind his bureau. He listened closely.

The type of scratching would reveal who had come through the passage.

Light scratching meant it was Eloise.

Heavy scratching meant it was Thaddeus.

Shane closed his eyes and tilted his head as he listened.

Thaddeus, Shane thought.

The scratching got louder and in another room he heard a bang.

The bureau hissed as Thaddeus pushed it out into the room.

The entry into the passageway was black.

Thaddeus breathed heavily in the dark.

"Go away," Shane said firmly.

The breathing grew heavier.

"Go away," Shane said again.

The toe of a worn boot protruded from the darkness.

"Go away!" Shane shrieked.

A second boot appeared, and the breathing became faster.

"I said, *go away!*" Shane screamed, and he launched himself from his bed. Yet he did not run for the safety of the hall and his parents' bed. Instead, he ran into the darkness, and he heard the surprise catch in Thaddeus' throat, and then Shane ran into the ghost.

Or rather, he ran through him.

Shane slammed headlong into the wall of the passage, and as he fell dizzily to the floor, Thaddeus rushed past him.

Enraged, Shane got to his feet and chased after the ghost.

Behind him, the passage slammed shut, and Shane was plunged into darkness.

His sudden inability to see caused him to stop. His rage quickly gave way to fear, and Shane realized he was trapped in the walls of the house with the dead.

He took a cautious step back, stumbled, fell and hit his head. Stars exploded in his eyes, and he struggled back to his feet. He couldn't tell which way would lead him back to his room.

He had no idea.

Cautiously Shane started to walk. He reached out both hands, so the fingers touched the rough wood of the narrow passage's walls. He took a few steps and pushed against the walls. He sought out a handle, one to open the door into his room.

He couldn't find anything, though.

He took a few more steps and tried again.

Nothing, he thought, and he realized he was going to be too afraid to do anything soon.

His breath started to race and he turned around again. He retraced his steps, sought out the handle, and when he didn't find it, he took a few more steps.

Still nothing.

Shane started to panic.

Something moved in the darkness behind him, and then a moment later another sound came from in front of him.

Shane sat down heavily, closed his eyes, put his hands over his ears, and he screamed.

He continued to scream until his voice hurt and his brain felt like it was going to explode.

His scream filled the small passage and soon he could feel rather than hear someone pound on the wall.

Shane stopped, put his hands down, and he heard, "Shane!"

It was his mother.

"Mom!" he screamed, crawling towards the part of the wall she had hit.

"Shane, stay where you are," she said firmly. "Your father's found an entrance in here, and he's getting the door open."

18

When the last syllable had slipped out of her mouth, a crack of bright light appeared a few feet from Shane on the left. He crawled to it. He panted as he reached the door. His mother leaned in, grabbed hold of him tightly and pulled him out into bright light.

Bright daylight.

She held onto him tightly, and Shane's father sat down heavily in a chair.

They were in the library on the second floor, across the house from Shane's room.

"How did you get here?" his mother asked, pushing him away slightly to look at him.

"I don't know," Shane said, sniffling back tears. "I don't know. I chased the ghost back into the passage, but then the door closed. I've been screaming. They were coming for me."

"Hank," she said, looking at his father.

"We've been looking for you," his father said. The man looked exhausted. "Your screams have been coming through every room in the house. We kept trying to find you."

"I want them all sealed up today, Hank," his mother said.

"I haven't even been able to check them all, Fiona," his father argued.

"I don't care," she snapped. "Close them up, Hank. Close them all up."

Shane's father opened his mouth to add something but closed it when he saw his wife's stare.

"Sure," his father grumbled. "Sure. I'll close them up today."

Chapter 8: In the House

The temperature in the house dropped steadily.

Soon Shane could watch each breath he exhaled. He stuffed his hands in his pockets and wandered absently through the front hallway. Pictures of himself and his parents hung on the walls. The photographs taken prior to their arrival at the house showed Shane as a little boy with a big smile.

After they had taken up residence on Berkley Street, however, his eyes had taken on a haunted look. His smile was not nearly as wide. His face was pale.

Life at the house had been difficult.

Shane paused at the bottom of the stairs and looked up.

His bedroom was at the top of the stairs and to the left. The closest room to his parents'. He could see how his door remained off the hinges, and he wondered if it was still propped up in the hallway of the servants' quarters or if someone had moved it.

Part of Shane wanted to go up the stairs and examine the rooms. In theory, no one had been in the house for nearly twenty years. Shane could smell a hint of death beneath the scent of lilacs, and he knew it wasn't new death. Not some animal trapped within the walls or a chimney. Nor was it an animal that had lived out its time and died.

The smell of death was the house's smell, no matter how much the ghosts had sought to mask it with lilacs.

Shane turned away from the stairs and walked to the front door. It was time for coffee with Gerald.

The knob turned easily in his hand, and he left his home. He didn't bother to lock the door.

The house would take care of itself.

Something flickered in the corner of his eye as he followed the driveway to where it met the road. As he walked along the stone wall which wrapped around his property on his right, Shane heard a noise.

Shane heard the whisper of someone's feet in the grass on the other side of the wall.

Whoever it was kept up with him and Shane didn't bother with questions. They would speak if they wanted to.

And they did.

"Where are you going?" a young man asked in German.

"To a neighbor's for coffee, Carl," Shane said, answering in kind.

"Come home soon, Shane," Carl said with a chuckle. *"We've missed you."*

Shane ignored the way his stomach twisted at the dead man's words. With a tired sigh he continued on his walk. It felt strange, Shane realized, to be in his old neighborhood. Some of the houses had changed, of course. Different colors and new roofs. None of it was so drastically altered, however, enough for him to not know exactly where he was. Soon, he found himself at Gerald's and he paused. The house in front of him was a well-built Victorian, a Painted Lady. The trim and clapboard, the spindles on the porch and the shutters on the windows, were all variations on the color purple.

The house's brilliant façade was stunning in the sunlight.

Shane felt oddly excited as he walked up to the front door and rang the bell.

From behind the door, he heard the electronic chime and the sudden, sharp bark of Turk.

A few moments later Gerald's voice came through the wood.

"Who is it?" the older man asked.

"Shane Ryan," Shane answered.

The deadbolt clicked, a small chain rattled, and the door opened.

Gerald smiled and stepped back. Turk sat a few feet away, and his tail thumped loudly on the old wooden floor. The house smelled strongly of coffee.

"Come in, Shane, come in. Here to take me up on my offer?" Gerald asked.

"I suppose I am," Shane said, stepping into the house. "I hadn't planned on it, but I suppose I am."

Gerald closed the door behind him and said, "Just go through the first door on your left. I've already got some coffee in there."

Shane nodded, turned left into the first room and took a seat in a high-backed leather arm chair. Gerald and Turk followed him in. Turk lay down in front of the fireplace, even though the hearth was unlit. Gerald walked to a small marble table, where a silver coffee urn stood.

A moment later, the older man carried the drink over to Shane, who nodded his thanks.

"My apologies, Shane," Gerald said as he sat down in a second leather armchair. "I don't take cream or sugar myself, so I tend not to have either one in the house, unless I know my kids are on their way to visit."

"No worries," Shane said. "I drink my coffee black."

Gerald nodded his approval and for a minute, the two men drank the warm, dark brew in silence.

"Well," Gerald said, "I have to ask. Why have you come back to the house now?"

"Like you said earlier," Shane said, "there was a bit of a dispute in regards to ownership. My aunt and uncle didn't feel it was right for an eighteen-year-old to own a house like mine."

Gerald frowned. "Why not?"

Shane shrugged, took a drink and said, "All I can think of is they wanted the house because of the trust fund. You see, my parents established a fund for the upkeep and care of the house, should anything happen to my dad. He wanted to make sure my mother would have a place to live. I don't think either of them expected it to go to me so quickly."

"So if your relatives had won ownership, they would have been able to live free in the house?" Gerald asked.

"Essentially," Shane said, nodding.

"And where were you going to live?"

Shane smiled. "My father and my Uncle Rick weren't close. In fact, they really didn't care for each other much at all. Uncle Rick and Aunt Rita really couldn't have cared less what happened to me after they got the house."

Gerald snorted derisively. "Mighty Christian of them."

"Funny you should mention Christian," Shane said. "Uncle Rick's a pastor at a place called the Holy Child Baptist Church down in Massachusetts."

Gerald laughed and shook his head. "Well, there's a fine joke for you."

Shane took a drink and then he grinned. "I don't much care for either of them. They tried to declare my parents dead, long before the legal time. They also pulled a lot of underhanded tricks. They hired a private investigator to see if I had something to do with the disappearance of my parents."

"Weren't you in boot camp at the time?"

Shane nodded.

Gerald snorted in disbelief, and Turk glanced up at him.

"Nothing to worry about, Turk," Gerald said, smiling at his dog. "Here's to you, Ryan, and welcome back to the neighborhood."

"Thank you."

"Will you be moving back in tonight?" Gerald asked.

Shane shook his head. "Tomorrow. I've got a few things to wrap up for work and then I'll take a few days off to get situated at home again."

"What do you do for work?" Gerald asked.

"I'm a freelance translator," Shane said. "Mostly non-fiction books. Military history stuff."

"You don't say?" Gerald said, nodding his head. "Impressive. What language?"

"Languages," Shane said, smiling. "German, French, Spanish, Italian. Just the basics."

"And you make good money, I assume?" Gerald asked, leaning back in his chair.

"Good enough," Shane answered. "And what about you, what did you do?"

"Worked in the defense industry. Perfected ways to kill people at a distance," Gerald said, shrugging. "There's no nice way to say it."

"No," Shane agreed, "there usually isn't."

Chapter 9: Shane, June 3rd, 1983

Shane sat in the back seat of the Cadillac, his arms crossed over his chest as he glared out the window.

His mother glanced back at him. "How was it?"

Shane looked at her, thought about something mean to say, but then turned and looked out the window again. He watched the trees of Greeley Park go by as his father guided the car towards home.

"Shane?" his mother said.

"I don't want to talk about it," Shane said.

"We're just curious is all, kid," his father said.

"I'm not crazy," Shane said, still looking out the window.

His father signaled to turn onto Swart Terrace.

"We didn't say you're crazy," his mother said quickly. "Dr. Wolfe doesn't think you're crazy either."

"Yes he does," Shane said. He looked at his mother. "He told me there aren't any such things as ghosts."

"Well come on, kid," his father said in a joking tone, "you know there aren't."

"I know what's in the house," Shane said angrily. "I know Eloise is dead. I know Thaddeus is dead. And there are others. They're in the walls. And there's the girl in the pond."

His parents looked at one another nervously and remained silent as his father turned into the driveway.

After the engine was shut off and they all got out and started to walk to the front door, Shane's mother asked, "Do you want to switch your bedrooms tonight?"

"It won't matter," Shane said.

"Why not?" his father asked.

"They don't care what room I'm in," Shane said, stepping over the threshold. "When they want to talk to me, they talk to me."

His mother tousled his hair as his father closed and locked the door.

"How do you know?" she said. "Don't you think they'll leave you alone if you're, say, in our room?"

Shane shook his head.

"No?" his father asked, chuckling. "Tell you what, kid, after dinner you can go to sleep in our room, and your mother and I will stay in there with you."

Eloise laughed from behind the grandfather clock, but Shane's parents didn't hear her.

"Sure," Shane said.

"Okay," the relief in his mother's voice was clear.

Shane went and played with his Star Wars figures in the kitchen while his mother got dinner ready. It was unusually hot for June according to Shane's father, so his mother heated hot dogs and baked beans while his father conducted some business over the telephone in the library.

Soon Shane had to put his toys away, and he ate dinner with his parents at the small table in the kitchen instead of the larger one in the dining room. His mother gave him a quick bath, got him into a pair of Superman pajamas, and soon he found himself in the middle of his parents' giant bed.

"What do you want to read tonight?" his father asked, leaning in the doorway as his mother sat down in the bed beside him.

"There's a Wocket in My Pocket!" Shane said, snuggling against his mother.

"Okay," his father said with a grin. He left the room and returned a minute later with the Dr. Seuss book. He carried it to a chair under the windows and then he brought the chair close to the bed. The evening sun poured in through the tall windows and filled the room with light.

Shane yawned, rolled a little in the cool sheets and pressed himself closer to his mother. He closed his eyes and listened to his father read.

Shane heard a soft hiss, and he opened his eyes.

The lights were off in his parents' room, the shades were drawn, and the sun had set a long time ago. He had fallen asleep while his father had read the book.

His parents liked to sleep with the door closed, so the room was dark.

The hiss sounded again, and it was quickly followed by a loud squeak.

"Shane," Eloise said.

He started to pant.

"Shane," she said again.

Another squeak sounded and something clattered on the floor.

"*Do you hear me, Shane?*" she asked, but it wasn't in English.

A different language. He didn't know what it was, but he *understood* it.

"*Yes,*" Shane said, answering in the same tongue. It came easily to him, as easily as English.

"*I want to play, Shane,*" she said, and something scratched across the floor.

"Hank," Shane's mother said tiredly.

A loud groan sounded.

"Oh, Jesus, Hank," his mother said, and Shane felt her sit up in the bed. Her hand stole out and found him.

"What?" he asked sleepily. "You okay, Fiona?"

The bed shifted slightly as his father sat up as well.

"What's going on?" he asked with a yawn.

The groan was followed by a scratch and a squeal.

Then something rushed across the hardwood floor and slammed into the doorframe.

"Damn it! Shane!" his father said angrily.

"He's in bed with us," his mother snapped.

"What?" he asked. "Watch your eyes."

Shane closed his eyes, and the light was turned on.

"Holy Mary Mother of God," he whispered.

Shane opened his eyes and saw his mother's long, dark brown chest of drawers pushed up against the door. Near the left corner of the room, one of the servants' doors had been opened. The thick coffin-head nails his father had used to close all of the doors lay on the floor. They were laid out in a neat row.

In the dark doorway stood three of Shane's small Star Wars action figures. Stormtroopers. Each of them had a blaster, and each blaster pointed at the bed.

"Shane," his father began.

"Hank," his mother said. "I've been holding onto him since I first heard a noise. He hasn't been out of this bed."

His father shook his head. "It doesn't make sense."

"Yes it does," Shane said, sinking back into the middle of the bed and looking up at the tin paneled ceiling.

"What do you mean?" his mother asked.

"Eloise is angry," Shane said, closing his eyes. "She wants to play with me, but you won't let her."

"Who's Eloise?" his mother said.

Shane opened his eyes and looked at her. "She's a little girl."

"And, and she's dead?" his mother asked.

"What killed her?" his father asked, and Shane could hear the doubt in his voice.

"The house did," Shane said.

"What?" his father asked, surprised. "What do you mean the house killed her?"

"The girl in the pond," Shane said. "She told the house to take Eloise, so it did."

"How do you know?" his mother asked.

"Eloise told me," Shane said.

"When?" his father asked.

"This morning," Shane said, closing his eyes and pulling the sheet up around him. "This morning. Where?" his father asked.

"In the butler's pantry," Shane answered. "There's another door in there."

His mother said something, but Shane couldn't quite make it out. Sleep stole over him, and he wondered what the dead would do next.

Chapter 10: Trespassing

Rick and Rita Ryan sat in their rented car a few houses down from the house which rightfully should have been theirs. Rick's obnoxious younger brother, Hank, had left everything to that spoiled brat Shane.

The same Shane, who had turned away a full scholarship to the Harvard Divinity School so he could join the Marines.

Shane, Rick and Rita agreed, was as stupid as Hank and Fiona had been.

And while Rick didn't particularly care for any of *those* people, he didn't particularly care as to where Hank and Fiona had disappeared to. At first, he had thought perhaps Hank had gotten himself into some financial trouble, and he and Fiona had taken off. It didn't explain the house, though, or why it was left to Shane.

After some thought, Rick and Rita had agreed Shane must have done something to his parents. In fact, they were positive and that somehow the boy had managed to convince the Marines and the government he was actually in South Carolina at basic training the whole time.

Rick knew better.

The boy had made his parents disappear.

It made perfect sense. The boy had been troubled ever since they had moved into the house. Rick and Hank's mother had told him so. Shane probably snuck back, murdered his parents and then he hid the bodies on his way back to South Carolina.

He was trained to be a killer, after all.

"There he is," Rita said.

Rick shook away his thoughts and looked to where Rita pointed.

Shane walked out of the yard, turned to the right and made his way up the street. Rick followed his nephew's progress until he crested a small rise and disappeared from view.

"Do you think he'll be gone long?" she asked, looking over at Rick.

"Has to be," Rick said confidently. "Kid doesn't even have a car. Must be walking to that hole of an apartment of his."

Rita nodded her agreement, pulled her peroxide blonde hair into a ponytail and asked, "Ready?"

"Yes, let's get it done," Rick said. He patted his coat pocket to make sure he had the car keys before getting out. Rita did the same, and a moment later they hurried across the street. They reached the sidewalk, crossed it and entered the property.

The first thing Rick noticed was the lack of noise.

No birds sang in the trees. No squirrels ran across the yard.

The house and everything around it were oddly silent.

Rita didn't seem to notice. She made a straight line for the front door.

Rick shook off his worries, hurried after her and caught up just as she turned the knob. Together, they entered the house.

"Good God," she said, "he left the place unlocked."

"What does he care?" Rick asked, closing the door behind him. "He didn't have to work for any of this. My brother did."

Rick swelled up self-righteously, and Rita gave him a pat on the arm.

"That's why we're here," she said proudly. "He doesn't deserve this stuff. Not the way you do."

Rick nodded in agreement.

The floor above them creaked as someone walked across it.

Rick saw Rita's eyes widen, and he felt his own do the same.

Behind them, the deadbolt clicked into place.

The room darkened, as though the sun was on a dimmer.

"Rick," Rita said uncomfortably. "No one's here, right?"

Rick shook his head. "Can't be. We watched this place all day, and the only one in or out was Shane."

All of the doors on the first floor slammed closed simultaneously, and the hallway was plunged into darkness.

Rita reached out and took hold of his arm. She pulled herself closer as she asked, "What the *hell* is going on, Rick?"

"I don't know," he answered.

And then someone took hold of his other arm. The grip was cold as it burned his flesh through his clothes.

"Yes, Rick," a soft, feminine voice said, "what is going on?"

"Oh, Jesus Christ protect us!" Rick yelled, ripping his arm out of the thing's grasp and stumbling into Rita.

"Who's here?" Rita demanded, tugging Rick closer to her.

The voice remained a short distance from them and chuckled. "A better question is, why are you here, in my house?"

The temperature sank quickly, and Rick shook with both chills and fear. Rita screamed and let go of his arm.

"Rita?!" Rick yelled, swinging his arms wide, trying to find his wife. His heart beat erratically and his breath came in great gasps. The panic attacks he had gotten a hold of decades earlier in his life came back, a great, terrible force. Waves of fear slammed into him, and he stumbled over his own feet. "Rita!"

"Not as lively as when she left you," the voice said. "No, not by far."

Rick turned away from the voice, stumbled into something heavy on the floor and fell headlong over it. He threw his hands out in front of him, his fingers broke and his knee crumpled as he landed. An involuntary scream was ripped out of his throat, and he groaned as he rolled onto his back.

A few feet away, a door opened, and a single, long rectangle of light spilled into the hallway.

It framed Rita perfectly.

Or what was left of Rita.

Her face was gone. Neatly removed, as though a surgeon had freed her of the burden of flesh. Her eyes were now lidless and stared straight up. An old porcelain doll sat beside his wife's mangled face. Its legs were spread, the dress it wore was a faded yellow and with expansive ruffles. The doll's blonde hair was neatly brushed and braided.

The doll looked at him, blinked, and grinned with bright white teeth.

Rick tried to look away, but brutally cold hands gripped his ears and forced his horrified gaze back to his wife's corpse.

"This house is not yours," the same feminine voice said from behind him. "It is mine. You were not invited in. You shall not be allowed out. But I think, dear Richard, you will live a little longer than your wife. Although you shall regret it."

And Rick screamed as the owner of the voice slowly peeled his ears from his head.

Chapter 11: Shane, November 6th, 1985

Shane lay in bed and listened to his parents argue.

He was sure they believed he was asleep, but they had woken him up.

He listened to the clock by his bed tick away the seconds, his father's voice clearly audible above it.

"I'm only saying it's a possibility, Fiona," he said.

"Really, Hank?" she said angrily. "Really? You're ready to think our son has some sort of supernatural, psychic abilities, but you won't admit to ghosts?"

"There's no evidence concerning ghosts," his father said defensively.

"Oh," his mother sneered, "and what 'evidence' is there about psychic phenomenon?"

"Lots," he snapped. "Places like Harvard and Yale, they're all doing tests in the field. It's documented. They can even repeat it in laboratory settings."

"So," she said. "You would rather believe our son has been doing all of this crap himself instead of thinking maybe, just maybe he might be right about the dead being here?"

"Come on, Fiona," his father said. Shane recognized the tone. It was the 'you know I'm right, let's not argue' tone Dad used to try to get his mother to calm down.

It never worked, and it didn't work this time either.

His mother got angrier.

"Shut up, *Henry*," his mother said.

Oh no, Shane thought. She had used his father's given name. The name he hated.

"Jesus Christ," he said. "We've never seen any of the stuff done. It's always when he's asleep or was about to sleep. It's definitely more in line with psychic abilities than it is with ghosts."

"What the hell is it going to take to get you to believe it?" she demanded.

"I need to know Eloise and Thaddeus were real," his father said defensively. "Prove to me they were real, and we can start to discuss the possibility of there being ghosts here."

Shane's mother said something Shane didn't quite catch, but he knew it wasn't pleasant. His dad didn't respond. He never responded when she said something really mean.

Evidence, Shane said to himself, closing his eyes. *I need to go to the library. I'll be able to get evidence there, I bet. The librarians know everything.*

Chapter 12: Shane, November 7th, 1985

It took Shane twenty-five minutes to walk from St. Christopher's School to the library, which was on Court Street, tucked behind the newspaper office and the canal. The air was cold, and he thought he might use the payphone to call his mom for a ride home when he was done.

It all depended on whether she was in a good mood or not.

She hadn't been angry with him before he left for school in the morning. She had even given him permission to go to the library. But she was definitely still mad about the argument with his dad, even though she didn't realize Shane had overheard most of it.

Maybe she still won't be mad at dad, he thought. He hurried to the library doors, pushed them open and walked in. Inside, it was wonderfully quiet.

He had been to the library several times with his mother and once with his father, but this was his first visit alone.

A pretty, older woman with black and white hair stood behind the long circulation desk. She punched date cards in a machine. The clunk of each stamp seemed entirely appropriate for the library.

After a moment, the librarian looked up, saw Shane and smiled.

"Good afternoon," she said. "May I help you?"

"I'm trying to look up the history of a house," Shane said. "Could you help me?"

"Well," the librarian said, putting the date cards down. "I can't, but we have a special librarian who knows how to find everything there is in the library. I'll bring you to her, okay?"

"Okay." Shane said, nodding.

"Good," the librarian said, "Follow me."

She walked down the length of the desk, and Shane kept pace with her as she headed towards a desk in the center of a larger room. An overhead sign said "Reference Desk" written on it in large red letters.

A woman much younger than the librarian, and possibly even younger than his mom, sat at the desk. A large, black bound book was open in front of her. She looked up over her glasses as Shane and the librarian approached.

"Tina," the woman smiled, inserting a slip of paper between the pages before closing it.

"Hello, Helen. This young man needs help finding out information on a particular house," Tina turned to Shane and said, "Good luck!"

"Thank you," Shane said, smiling.

"So you need help?" Helen asked.

"Yes, ma'am. I do," Shane answered.

"Excellent. You are in the right place, young man," she said with a grin. "Now, what house do you want to know about?"

"My house," Shane said. "I live at one twenty-five Berkley Street."

The smile on Helen's face dropped away. She cleared her throat uncomfortably and asked, "Did you say one twenty-five Berkley Street?"

"Yes, ma'am," Shane said.

Helen's skin grew pale. She licked her lips nervously. "How long have you lived there?"

"A couple of years," Shane said.

"Oh," she said. "I grew up on Chester Street."

"Hey," Shane said with a smile, "Chester Street is right next to Berkley."

Helen nodded. She managed a small smile and then asked him, "So, what would you like to know about your house?"

Shane grew serious. "I'd like to know if anyone ever died at my house."

For a long moment, Helen didn't answer and Shane was worried he had asked an inappropriate question.

Finally, she took a deep breath and asked, "Why do you want to know if someone died in the house? What's happened?"

Shane looked at her and whispered, "You know, don't you."

Helen opened her mouth to reply, closed it, and then she nodded. "Yes. Yes, I do know."

"How?" he asked her.

She glanced around before she leaned forward and said, "I went in, once, when I was a little girl."

"What did you see?" Shane asked.

"When my parents were talking with Mrs. Anderson I was allowed to play in her parlor. The room was dark, and out of the shadows, I heard another little girl."

"Eloise," Shane whispered.

Helen nodded her head. "Yes. Eloise. We talked for a while. She wouldn't come out of the shadows. She didn't want to scare me. I thought she had something wrong with her. After a little while, she went away, and I went into the kitchen. I told my parents and asked how long Mrs. Anderson's granddaughter was visiting."

"Eloise lives there," Shane said. "She never leaves."

"No," Helen said. "She never leaves."

"Did she die there?" Shane asked.

"Yes," Helen said, nodding. "Yes, she did. I'm not sure how. No one is. There is a small book, in the Stearns Room, about your house. Are you old enough to read it?"

Shane nodded.

Helen looked at him closely for a minute and then she stood up. "Yes. I think you are, too. Come with me. I'm sorry, I didn't even ask you your name."

"I'm Shane Ryan," Shane said, extending his hand the way his father had taught him.

Helen smiled and shook it. "Helen McGill. Follow me, Shane."

She led him to the back of the library, along the rear wall to a room guarded by a pair of large, wooden doors. She took a key ring out of her pocket, unlocked the door and pushed it open. A tall room was revealed. Bookshelves were protected by glass fronts and narrow windows looked out over the canal's small waterfall. A long table, occupied by half a dozen leather chairs, stood in the room's center.

Helen turned on the light, walked over to a bookcase and slid the glass protector out of the way. She bent down, reached in and withdrew a slim book. Helen looked at it briefly before she stood up and walked to the table.

"Sit down, Shane," she said, pulling out a chair for herself. Shane sat down at the table beside her.

She put the book down and opened it.

Shane leaned forward and saw a black and white picture of his house beside a faded picture of a different, smaller house.

"This house," Helen said, tapping the picture of the strange home, "was at one twenty-five Berkley Street before yours. The Andersons purchased the property in nineteen thirty, and then they added on and changed it into the one you live in now."

"When was the first one built?" Shane asked.

Helen turned the page to 'Chapter I.'

"According to whoever wrote this," she said, "the original house was built in eighteen-fourteen. It was sold several times and each time the house was changed just a little bit. Things were added on."

She turned the page to a curious illustration.

"Do you see this?" she asked, tracing a thick line with her finger.

"Yes," Shane said.

"Each wide line is a secret corridor," Helen said. "As the house was built, and wealthier people bought it, they made sure their servants couldn't be seen. The servants were able to walk to any room in the house without bothering the owners. And that was the way they wanted it. By the time the Andersons bought and finished the house to the way it is now, they made sure the doors the servants used couldn't even be noticed when they were closed."

Shane nodded. "I know. It's terrible. My father thinks he sealed all of the doors, but we keep finding them."

Helen looked at him, swallowed nervously and said, "I'm going to tell you a secret, Shane, okay?"

"Yes," he answered.

"The house makes more doors," she said in a low voice. "Eloise told me all those years ago."

"Helen," Shane said nervously, "do you know who Thaddeus is?"

Helen's hands shook, and she turned several pages to another picture.

Shane looked at an old photograph of a boy about his own age. The boy wore an old-fashioned suit, worn boots and he smiled at the camera. He held a small rifle in his hands and behind him was the pond at Shane's house.

Shane knew it was the pond because he could see the dead girl in it. The girl with no name who stayed right below the surface and watched him in the yard.

"Do you see her?" Helen whispered.

Shane nodded.

"Not everyone does," Helen said, closing the book on the disturbing photograph. "Thaddeus swallowed some water while swimming in the pond and later, when he fell asleep, he died. They call it dry drowning. A little water in the lungs is enough to kill."

"She killed him," Shane said. It wasn't a question, and Helen didn't take it as one.

"She did," Helen agreed. "I can remember looking at the pond as a little girl. Mrs. Anderson made sure I never was allowed near it. Sometimes, from my window, I could see the fish swimming in the water, or the watermen near the edges. Once in a great while ducks would land on the water, but they'd fly away soon after, and there'd always be a dead duck floating."

"She doesn't like ducks," Shane said, nodding. "I've seen a couple of dead ducks before my dad fishes them out. He says they died naturally, but I know she killed them. I don't know why, though."

Shane looked at her. "Could you do me a favor, Helen?"

"What is it?" she asked.

"Could you write down the names of Eloise and Thaddeus for me, and when they died?" he said.

"Sure," she said, slightly confused. "Why?"

"My dad doesn't believe there are ghosts in the house," Shane answered. "He thinks I'm the one who keeps moving things around."

Helen frowned. "Does your mom believe you?"

Shane nodded. "He said he might believe in ghosts if my mother could prove people had died in the house."

"A lot of people have died at one twenty-five Berkley Street, Shane," Helen said in a grim voice. "Eloise and Thaddeus are only two of them."

Shane sighed and said, "I was afraid so."

Chapter 13: Whispers in the Walls

Something was wrong.

Shane could feel it.

With the morning sun on his back and his few possessions in the truck he had rented, Shane stood in the open doorway.

The house felt *wrong*. It smelled wrong.

Blood, Shane thought. *I can smell blood.*

His hands itched to hold a glass of whiskey as he stepped into the house and walked forward. The sun shined down into the rooms off the hallway, and some of the light spilled out onto the beautiful hardwood floor.

And Shane saw the stain. Not a large stain, just a few drops a dozen steps in. He walked slowly to the spot and crouched down.

Blood, Shane thought. He reached out and touched it. It was dry. He straightened up and looked around.

Whispers came from behind the massive grandfather clock and as Shane took a step towards it, the pendulum started to swing. The hands moved backward, playfully.

"Eloise," Shane said.

A giggle sounded, and the whispers stopped.

The clock's hands changed directions.

"Eloise," Shane said again.

"Hello Shane," Eloise said, her voice slightly muffled. "You've been gone a very long time."

"I know," Shane said. Fear crawled up his legs and settled in his stomach.

"Why?" Eloise asked, tapping on the wall on either side of the clock.

The noise brought back memories of his childhood and Shane shivered.

"I wasn't allowed." Shane said. He cleared his throat. "Did anyone come in here yesterday?"

"Yes," Eloise answered.

"Did they leave?" Shane asked.

"No," she said.

"Well," Shane said, anger slowly replacing his fear, "where are they, Eloise?"

"Here," she said. "In the walls, and in the basement. In the attic and in the pond."

"How many people came in?" he asked.

"Two," Eloise said.

Shane closed his eyes and took a deep breath. A moment later he opened them and asked, "What happened to them?"

"Carl happened to them," Eloise said cheerfully.

Shane's breath caught in his throat. "Carl."

"Carl," she repeated. "We've all missed you so much, Shane. Where will you be sleeping tonight? In your room?"

"Yes," Shane said softly, turning to look back at the stain on the floor. "Yes. Where else would I sleep?"

For the briefest of moments, he wondered who had died at the hands of Carl, and then he pushed the thought away.

I'll find out soon enough, he sighed. He turned around and headed for the door. He needed to bring his things in.

Chapter 14: Shane, December 12th, 1985

Shane's father finally believed in ghosts.

It wasn't because Shane had gotten the information from Helen, the librarian. It wasn't because his mother had double checked the information with Helen, the librarian. It wasn't even his father going down himself to the library.

No. It wasn't any of those.

It was what had happened in the morning. Down at the pond.

The weather had been a little warmer, and the sun and wind had cleared the snow from the surface of the pond. The ice, revealed, shined brightly, and his father had wondered if he could see the fish under the ice.

Shane had stood a safe distance away from the pond. He didn't trust it. Especially after Helen had told him about Thaddeus.

So Shane stood in snow that covered up to the tops of his moon boots. He moved his toes around and listened as the Wonderbread bags on his feet crinkled. The bags were an extra layer of warmth and protection, insisted upon by his mom.

Shane pretended to smoke and exhaled great clouds of his breath into the air as he watched his dad, who crept carefully out onto the ice.

Shane's mother had left the house earlier, shortly after he got home from school, to get the groceries. His father had been home since a furnace technician had come out and double checked the furnace and the oil line. If his mother hadn't gone to get food, then Shane's father never would have gone out on the ice.

She wouldn't have let him.

Shane's father knew it as well, and he had sworn Shane to secrecy.

Shane had agreed, but he also knew if his father did something foolish he'd have to tell his mom.

Shane didn't want to disappoint his mother, and a lie would upset her.

"Oh damn!" his father yelled, and Shane watched as his father suddenly sank to his knees in the pond, the ice cracking loudly beneath him.

"Dad!" Shane cried out.

"I'm okay," his father said, twisting around to face Shane. He forced a smile. "I'm just freezing and wet. I'll be fine."

The smile vanished though, and he stumbled back. A look of pure terror filled his face as he struggled towards the shore. He jerked back again, and he looked down, let out a terrified scream and practically ran out of the pond.

Shane stepped towards him, and he pointed back to the house.

"Inside!" his father yelled. "Inside now!"

Something sickly and white reached up out of the water from behind him.

Shane turned and sprinted for the basement door. Behind him, he heard heavy footsteps crash through the snow. Just as Shane made it inside, his father rushed in behind him and slammed the door shut.

The man breathed raggedly and shook from head to toe. Water dripped from his jeans and leaked out of his boots. Shane watched him take cautious steps to the washer and dryer, strip down and then dig a pair of sweats and fresh socks out of a wicker laundry basket. Within a minute, he was dressed, and he left his wet clothes where they lay.

"Come on, Shane," his father said hoarsely. "Let's go upstairs."

Shane kicked off his snow gear, pulled the bread bags off of his feet, and dutifully went up into the kitchen. His dad opened a cabinet, took out some alcohol and poured himself a large drink. Shane rarely saw him with alcohol, and he had never seen him upend a glass and empty it in one gulp.

His father's hands shook as he put the glass on the counter.

For a long, silent minute he gripped the edge of the counter and looked down at the sink.

"I'm sorry," he said after a minute. "I'm sorry, Shane."

"Why?" Shane asked.

His father turned and faced him, his lips pressed tightly together and nearly white. "For not believing you about ghosts. About the ghosts here."

"What did you see?" Shane asked in a low voice.

"A girl," he answered quickly. "I saw a girl in the pond. She grabbed my leg. She tried to pull me in."

The man turned back to the glass and the bottle and poured himself another drink.

"I'm sorry," his father whispered, and Shane nodded as the glass was emptied again.

Chapter 15: Why He Returned

Shane was afraid.

He sat in his old bed, a book beside him. His cigarettes and lighter stood beside his bottle of whiskey and a tumbler. Shane had made sure to move the bureau away from the servants' door. He had removed the nails from every door he could find.

Soon Shane would have to speak with them. Almost all of them.

And he didn't want them in a bad mood.

They're grumpy enough as it is, he thought with a sigh.

He looked down at his book, *The Moon is Down*, by John Steinbeck, and he wondered idly if he could concentrate enough to read. He doubted it, and he doubted they would give him the opportunity.

Eloise was pleased he had returned. Carl was happy he had come back. And the old man, well, who knew with the old man.

The real question, however, was whether or not Shane would be allowed to find his parents. Or at least, learn what had happened to them.

Shane leaned back against his pillows and looked at the lights in his room. He had three of them plugged in, as well as his fan which droned on slowly as it oscillated from left to right and back again. For decades, the lights and fan had helped him sleep. In the Marines, he had been too exhausted to not sleep well. On the rare occasions where sleep attempted to avoid him, well, the raucous noise of his Marine brethren had lulled him into rest.

Shane closed his eyes, listened to the white noise of the fan and waited.

He didn't know if he had fallen asleep or if they had waited only for him to seem at rest. Regardless as to what occurred, his thoughts were brought back into focus by the strained squeak of the servants' door.

Memories of childhood, of his screams as they ricocheted off walls, it all came back to him with brutal force. The fear evoked by the hidden portal was visceral and primal. Shane was no longer a man of forty returned to his parents' home, but a child of eight, trapped in the Star Wars sheets of his bed.

Shane forced himself to keep his eyes closed. Silently he counted the seconds as they dragged by, carried along with the scratching of his old bureau on the wood floor.

Seven seconds exactly and the noise ceased.

"Shane," Eloise said.

"Hello, Eloise," Shane replied, keeping his eyes closed.

"Why won't you look at me?" she asked playfully. "Are you afraid, Shane?"

"Always," he answered truthfully.

The dead girl laughed and a boy asked, "Why have you come back to us, Shane?"

Thaddeus, Shane thought. "I need answers," he said aloud. "I need to know where my parents are, Thaddeus."

"Hmph," Thaddeus said, and Shane could picture the dead boy's frown. "Your parents are exactly where she wants them to be."

"Who is 'she'?" Shane asked, his heart beating excitedly.

"The girl in the pond," Eloise whispered. "She is she."

"Yes," Thaddeus said. "She likes your parents where they are. They're nearly quite mad, you know."

Shane stiffened and opened his eyes.

As he did so, the lights flicked out, and the fan stopped. Shane's breathing was terribly loud.

The room was black, too dark for him to see anything.

But he could smell them. The stale air odor which lingered about the two children. He knew it well.

"May I see my parents?" he managed to ask after peered into the darkness for a moment.

"You may," Thaddeus said, chuckling, "or you may not. It is her decision, Shane. Not ours."

"How do I ask her permission?" Shane asked.

Neither of the ghosts answered him.

"How do I ask for permission?" Shane snapped, trying to keep the rage and excitement out of his voice.

"You don't want to ask, Shane," Eloise whispered. "You don't ever want to talk to her."

"No," Thaddeus agreed. "Best to forget about your parents, for now, Shane. They will keep, and you must as well. Not everyone is pleased to see you've returned."

Chapter 16: Investigation

Detective Marie Lafontaine stood on the corner of East Stark Street and Berkley Street. She adjusted her scarf and looked out at Berkley Street, first to the left, and then to the right.

In Brighton, Massachusetts, a middle-aged woman had reported her parents missing. Richard and Rita Ryan. Ages sixty-seven and sixty-eight respectively. Both were recently retired. Richard had sold his share of his wife's family's car dealership, at a loss, to pay for a decades-long legal battle which he had lost.

A legal battle over the property of his missing, and legally declared dead brother.

A black Toyota Nissan Sentra, rented to Mr. Ryan, had been found abandoned on East Stark Street. The car had faced the house which Mr. Ryan and his wife had so recently lost the battle for.

The car had been ticketed twice for being parked overnight. Finally, an alderman who lived on Berkley Street had called to complain. The car was towed to the impound lot, its information put through the system, and Mr. Ryan's information had popped up. Another cross-check showed the man and Rita were listed as missing persons.

The discovery of the car, parked so close to the house, brought with it a concern of foul play. Especially since ownership of the house had been so heavily contested and for such a lengthy period of time.

The house was now owned and occupied by Shane Ryan, son of Hank and Fiona Ryan, who had mysteriously vanished while Shane was in South Carolina at Marine Corps basic training.

Marie looked at the house and felt uncomfortable, sickened.

Something was wrong with it. Something was off. She wasn't quite sure what it was, but she could feel it. A knife blade of doubt and fear in her stomach.

Marie opened the door of the unmarked Impala, leaned in and took the microphone out of its cradle. She keyed it.

"Base this is Four Three," she said.

"Four Three this is Base, go."

"Base, approaching number one two five Berkley Street for interview."

"Good copy, Four Three, check back in five."

"Copy, out," she said.

Marie hung the microphone back up and closed the door. She pushed aside her jacket, adjusted the volume on her handheld radio, and crossed Berkley Street. She walked directly to the front door of the house, rapped on it sharply, and waited.

Several moments passed and she raised her hand to knock again when the sound of a lock's tumbler interrupted her. She lowered her arm and took a cautious step-down.

The door opened, and an exhausted-looking man answered the door. She estimated him to be in his late thirties, perhaps a hundred and fifty pounds and almost five ten. Her critical eye roved over him and identified his worn and faded blue jeans, a patched black sweater, and new running shoes. He lacked any sort of hair from what she could see. Not by choice, but by a physical ailment.

"May I help you?" the man asked politely.

Marie nodded. "Mr. Ryan? I'm Detective Lafontaine with the Nashua Police Department, I was wondering if I could ask you a few questions?"

"Sure," he said, stepping aside. "Come on in. Too cold out to chat on the front step."

"Thank you," Marie said as she walked into the massive foyer. She kept her reactions under control, but she was impressed at the size of the house. It looked even bigger on the inside than it did from the street, and the house was huge when viewed from the curb.

"So," Mr. Ryan said. "What can I help you with, Detective?"

"I'm here because a car your aunt and uncle rented was found nearby," Marie said.

Shane frowned. "You mean Rick and Rita Ryan?"

"Yes," she said.

"I don't know why it would be," he said. "I haven't spoken to either of them since my grandmother's funeral in nineteen eighty-seven."

"So you haven't seen either one of them?"

He shook his head. "No. We're not exactly on good terms. They know they wouldn't be welcome here."

"Why exactly?" Marie asked, although she already knew the answer.

"They wanted my parents' house," Mr. Ryan said, gesturing at the home. "They've been trying to get it since my parents disappeared over twenty years ago."

"They've been trying to get you out of the house?" she asked.

Mr. Ryan chuckled and shook his head. "No. I haven't been living here. Not in the house. Because of the legal issues the house has been empty."

"Where have you been living?" Marie said.

"On Locust Street. Little studio apartment," he answered.

"And do you live here alone?" she asked.

Mr. Ryan nodded.

"Do you work outside of the house?"

"No," he said. "I do freelance translating. All of my work is done online. I walk a bit each day, but otherwise, I spend most of my time indoors."

"Is your car in the shop?" Marie asked. "I didn't see it outside."

"I don't own a car," he replied. "I don't like to drive."

Marie glanced around the hallway and then she asked, "When did you move in?"

"Three days ago," he said.

"The house is spotless," Marie said, registering a curious looking splatter on the wood floor. "Did it take you a long time to clean it?"

"What do you mean?" he asked.

"You said the house was empty this whole time," Marie said, smiling. "There must have been a lot of dust."

"No," Mr. Ryan said with a shake of his head. "There wasn't. The house takes care of itself. I didn't have to clean anything."

"Oh," she said. *This place has been scoured. He's full of it. Someone's been cleaning.*

Her nose wrinkled slightly at a metallic smell. *Old blood?* She thought. Marie smiled and offered her hand and he shook it. "Well, thank you for your time, Mr. Ryan."

Marie took a business card out of her wallet and handed it to him. "This is my number at the station, Mr. Ryan. Please call me immediately if you hear from either your aunt or your uncle."

The man nodded his head as he took it. He held it loosely in one hand and walked her to the door. He opened it for her and nodded good-bye.

When Marie reached the sidewalk, she keyed her radio and said, "Four Three to Base."

"Go ahead Four Three, this is Base."

"Finished at one two five Berkley Street. En route to station."

"Good copy, Four Three."

"Four Three out."

Marie returned the radio to her belt and glanced back at the house.

In the far, upper right window a young man watched her carefully.

She waved, and he waved in return.

Marie turned away and thought, *He said he lived alone.*

She would have to check out some of what Mr. Ryan had said, and learn why the house stank of blood.

Chapter 17: The Little Place of Forgetting, August 1st, 1986

Shane sat in the library on the second floor of his house. He usually didn't go into the library. Neither did his parents. The room had come fully stocked with books, but they weren't anything his parents had ever been interested in reading. The library was usually off limits, since his mother had a 'weird feeling' about it.

When Shane had woken up a few hours earlier, the rain had poured down from dark clouds. His father had left for work, and his mother had gone to visit a friend, and Shane had been given permission to stay at home.

Which was better than a visit to Mrs. Murray, where his mother would spend the better part of the day.

Shane had wanted to finish the tank model he had started the night before. Unfortunately, he had left the cap off of the glue, so he couldn't complete it. He couldn't paint it either since he had forgotten to buy new paints.

For about an hour he had wandered around the house and tried to stay out of most of the rooms. Eloise had loosened a few of the doors, and he could hear her in the walls. The old man who lived in his parents' bathroom had filled the second floor with groans for most of the morning.

The only room Shane hadn't been into was the library.

And so he had gone there to escape Eloise and the old man, Thaddeus and some of the others whose names he didn't know. He wasn't afraid of them, at least not during the day. At nighttime, he was terrified, but it wasn't his fault. They opened doors constantly.

The only one he was afraid of during the daytime was the girl in the pond. The unnamed girl. The one who had tried to drown his father, and who always got closer to the surface when Shane was in the backyard.

So, in an effort to avoid the wanderers in the walls and the murderer in the water, Shane had decided to visit the library.

And he was *thrilled*.

The previous owner had been Mr. Anderson. Shane's father said the man had filled the library with books. They were great books. Books all about wars and military and history.

All of the things Shane loved to read about. Most of the books were old. Some of them printed in foreign languages, and there were dictionaries for all the languages too. Shane could figure out what they were about if he wanted to.

When the clock on the library's mantle struck ten, Shane stretched. On the floor in front of him was a German to English dictionary. Beside it was a slim book. Shane had figured out the title.

Letters of German Students in the World War.

It had taken him a long time.

A cool breeze suddenly ran along Shane's back.

He twisted around to see what it was.

All he could see were bookshelves.

And it didn't feel the same as when Eloise or Thaddeus moved past him.

He held his hand out and felt the cold air against his skin. He moved his hand a little to the left, and the breeze disappeared. Back to the right and he found it again.

Shane twisted around and started to follow the air. Soon he felt it on his face, and it seemed to issue forth from a bookshelf. When he reached it, Shane touched the books on the shelves and found only the ones on the bottom shelf were cold.

A secret door, Shane thought. He was excited. This wasn't a secret door the dead had told him about. Or one his father had found. No one knew about it but himself.

Shane stood up, and he looked at the bookshelf carefully. Then he found what he sought, a small, smooth bump at the back of the center shelf. He reached in and pushed on it.

A loud click sounded, and the whole bookcase swung out half an inch.

Excited, Shane took hold of the edge and pulled it back. The whole thing moved easily and silently.

Behind it, a tall, dark wood door was revealed. A slim metal handle protruded, and Shane grabbed it. He twisted up and down, but the door didn't budge. Then he pulled it to the left, and the door slid on tracks into the wall. A hole was revealed, set within the floor. The walls were smooth, a push-button light switch the only thing marring the surface.

Shane turned the light on and down the length of the hole, lights flickered into life. Electric bulbs in wire cages.

Shane leaned forward slightly and looked down.

Perhaps twenty or so feet down, he saw a skeleton, clad in a suit, and curled up on the floor of the hole.

Shane shivered, turned off the light and closed the door. He looked at the bookcase as he was about to close it and saw something written on the backside of it.

My Oubliette, the first sentence said. *My little place of forgetting. I shall forget he existed, and so shall the world.*

Shane's hands shook as he closed the secret door and he wondered who the person was.

Chapter 18: Carl and the Remembering

Once more Shane sat in his room.

He had found the picture, which his parents had hidden from him in his father's sock drawer when he was fourteen.

The photograph was in a tramp art frame, a cunning piece of woodwork made from scraps. Some man had crafted it in the Great Depression and made it as a gift for Mrs. Anderson. The picture within was older than the frame, and the photo was of a handsome young man in a German uniform. The photograph had been taken at some point during the First World War, and the man's name had been Carl Hesselschwerdt.

A Stormtrooper, a skilled soldier who had survived four years of combat before he suffered a wound and had been captured by American Marines. Eventually, Carl had immigrated to the United States shortly after the economic collapse in America. He had been a scholar, had come to New Hampshire, and then he had disappeared.

Vanished until Shane had found his remains in nineteen eighty-seven, at the bottom of the oubliette. It had taken Shane a long time to find Carl's picture, to find out who the dead man had been.

Shane made sure to remember, and Carl loved him for it.

And now Shane sat in his room and waited for Carl to visit.

A flicker of light announced the dead man's arrival.

A moment later Shane caught a glimpse of Carl in the slim shadow along the wall by the closet.

"How nice it is to have you home, Shane," Carl said in German.

"It is, in a way, nice to be home again, my friend," Shane said, replying in German. It was a curious sensation to know he was now older than Carl had ever been.

Carl stepped out of the shadows. He was slim and rather short, but the suit he wore was well-cut, the shoes glowed with a curious light, and Shane had to remind himself the man was dead. Had been for eighty years.

And Carl, for some unknown reason, was vicious when he wanted to be.

Carl looked to the bed table, saw his own photograph and smiled. Shane remembered the night his parents had taken the photo away. Carl had been displeased, and his parents had not slept well.

Not for a long time.

In spite of their belief in ghosts, neither his mother nor his father believed Shane when he had told them Carl wanted his image placed in the open again.

"Thank you, my friend," Carl said. *"Thank you for remembering."*

"Always," Shane said, smiling. *"I was wondering if perhaps you could assist me, Carl."*

"Of course. How?"

"I am seeking a way to find my parents," Shane said.

Carl looked at him for a long moment before he answered.

"I can show you the entrance," Carl said hesitantly, *"but it will be dangerous for you. Not nearly as dangerous as it was for them, yet it will be dangerous nonetheless."*

Shane nodded.

"We had a bit of trouble, several days ago, Shane," Carl said.

Shane frowned. *"What sort of trouble?"*

"Your aunt and uncle," Carl replied. *"They came in uninvited."*

The image of the blood on the floor and the stink of it in the air flashed before Shane's eyes. *"Carl, did you do something to them?"*

"I did."

Shane took a deep breath and asked, *"What, my friend, did you do to them?"*

"I killed them."

"And their bodies?" Shane managed to ask.

"Within the oubliette."

"The police were here," Shane said. *"They will return."*

"They will not find the bodies."

"I saw the evidence," Shane started to say.

Carl held up a hand. *"The old man has scrubbed the floor, and the dark ones have hidden the scent."*

56

Shane shivered at the mention of the dark ones. He had blessedly forgotten them. The little, half-seen things, the unknown dead who scurried from shadow to shadow even in the brightest part of the day.

"It is through them you must pass," Carl said, and not without compassion.

"What do you mean?" Shane asked, a cold sweat erupting across his brow.

"The domain of the dark ones. The root cellar. Beneath the butler's pantry. Your parents heard them, and down they went," Carl said.

Shane felt sick to his stomach.

"The root cellar," Shane whispered. *"They went into the root cellar."*

Carl nodded.

In English Shane said, "I told them not to."

"I know."

"I told them never to go into the root cellar. I told them to board it up. To buy cement, to fill it."

"I know, my friend," Carl said sadly.

"Are they here? Are they dead?" Shane asked, switching back to German.

"She will not tell us."

"Will she tell me?" Shane said.

Carl took a nervous step back. *"You cannot, Shane. No one speaks with her."*

"I have to know."

"Then go to the root cellar," Carl said grimly. *"You will have a better chance there than with her."*

Shane's heart beat so loudly, the sound of it nearly drowned out his own breath as it raced in and out of his lungs. *"I'll have to, won't I?"*

"I cannot go with you," Carl said, fear thick in his voice. *"I went down once for you."*

"I know," Shane said, smiling tightly. *"I know. And I thank you for it. I do not ask you to come, Carl."*

Shane let out a shaky laugh.

"You will wait until the morning?" Carl asked.

"I will."

"Will you speak with me?" Carl said. *"It has been a long time since I have had the pleasure of your company."*

"Yes," Shane said, nodding. *"Yes. It has been far too long."*

"When last we spoke you were joining the United States Marine Corps," Carl said. *"Tell me, how was it? Did you taste the bitter draught of war, my young friend?"*

"I did," Shane answered. *"And I would rather be in combat than preparing to descend the ladder into the root cellar."*

He looked at Carl, pleased to have the ghost with him once more. After a moment he said in a low voice, *"I'm afraid, Carl."*

The dead man nodded. *"You should be, Shane. You should be."*

Chapter 19: Shane, October 1st, 1986

Shane was alone in the house.

Specifically, he was alone in the butler's pantry. He glanced at the boxes of dry goods, the different cans of soup and vegetables, some bags of chips, some of his father's beer and his mother's wine.

Shane focused his attention on the far left corner, though. The dark shadow where the servants' door remained hidden. He stood perfectly still and waited.

Soon, the door opened.

It swung out into the room, and an ancient hinge screamed. Shane winced and turned his head slightly. Someone spoke, and Shane strained to understand the words.

"What do you want, child?" a man asked in German. Shane had been studying the language from the books found in the library. But for some reason, he found he understood a great deal of it, especially when he heard people speak it.

"I wanted to talk to you," Shane said hesitantly. He shifted the picture he had hidden behind his back from one hand to the next, the wooden pyramids on the frame smooth beneath his skin.

The ghost snorted. *"About what would you have me speak, child?"*

"I found something," Shane said, pausing between words to make sure he was speaking correctly. He remembered the skeleton at the bottom of the oubliette. He recalled what had been written on the door, how the dead man would be forgotten.

From behind his back, Shane pulled the photograph in the curious wooden frame. A photograph of a young man in a soldier's uniform. He had seen the ghost before. He recognized his lean face in the younger man's.

The dead man said nothing for a long time.

Shane's hands shook as he held the picture out and waited to see what would happen.

Finally, the ghost asked in a whisper, *"Where did you find it, child?"*

"*In the parlor,*" Shane answered. "*It was on a low shelf, by the fireplace. I almost didn't see it.*"

He stepped out of the darkness and once more Shane recognized the suit he had seen at the bottom of the oubliette. The ghost looked up from the photograph to Shane and asked, "*Would you like to know my name?*"

"Yes," Shane said.

"*I am Carl Wilhelm Hesselschwerdt, and I was murdered by Mr. Anderson,*" he said.

"*I'm sorry,*" Shane responded.

Carl smiled. "*You've no need to be sorry, Shane. You will remember me?*"

Shane thought of the lonely skeleton and the horrible thing Mr. Anderson had written, and Shane nodded. "*I'm going to put the picture by my bed.*"

"*Thank you,*" Carl said with a sigh. "*Thank you.*"

Chapter 20: The Morning Arrives

While the nightmares had not gotten worse with his return to the house, they had not gotten any better either.

Shane put his toothbrush back, ran his hand over his bald head, and left the bathroom. He went to his bedroom, poured himself a second shot of whiskey and downed it quickly. For a moment, he contemplated a third, but then he put the tumbler back on his bed table. Shane made his way to the kitchen to make some breakfast.

Dishes rattled in the cabinets and Shane sighed.

"Why are you here?" the old man asked, his voice seeming to come from all corners of the room at once.

"To eat breakfast," Shane said.

"I'll not accept sass, young man," the old man said, and the empty chairs at the table shivered.

"Don't ask stupid questions," Shane replied. He wasn't in any mood for the old man's harassment.

"What are you doing back at the house?" the old man said. "I am curious. Tell me why."

"I want to find my parents," Shane said, taking a drink of coffee.

"Ask her," the old man said, chuckling. "Ask her what she's done with them."

"You ask her," Shane said, cutting the ghost's laughter short.

The doorbell rang.

Shane frowned and looked at the clock on the stove.

Six thirty.

He took a bite of his toast, washed it down with a bit more of his coffee and stood up. He made his way to the front door and had just about reached it when the bell rang again.

Shane rolled his eyes at the sound, waited for it to finish and then he said through the door, "Who is it?"

"Mr. Ryan," a woman said. "This is Detective Lafontaine, and I'm here with a warrant to search your premises."

Shane groaned inwardly, undid the locks and opened the door.

Detective Lafontaine stood on the doorstep with a dozen other police officers and forensic personnel behind her. They all looked terribly serious.

For a moment, Shane had an urge to crack a joke, but he resisted.

Detective Lafontaine had an extremely severe look on her attractive face, and Shane wondered what she might look like when she wasn't being a police officer. In her hand, she held a warrant, which she offered to him. Shane nodded, accepted it, and stepped out of their way. She came in and stood beside him as he opened the warrant and read it.

Any and all evidence relating to the disappearance of Richard Michael Ryan and Rita Joan (Sanderson) Ryan, Shane saw.

Of course, he thought, managing to keep his sigh bottled up. *Of course.*

"Mr. Ryan," the detective said. "Is there anything you'd like to tell us before we begin searching the house?"

"No," Shane said honestly. "But I am going to go back to the kitchen and finish my breakfast. You're welcome to join me for a cup of coffee. Any of you are."

He folded the warrant and tucked it into his back pocket. Detective Lafontaine followed him into the kitchen.

"Do you want coffee, Detective?" he asked.

"Yes please," she said, shrugging off her coat and hanging it on the back of one of the chairs.

Shane brought down a mug, filled it and handed it to her.

"Sorry," he said, setting it down on the table, "I don't have cream or sugar."

"Thank you," she said with a polite smile. "I drink it black."

Shane returned the smile, politely, and sat down.

"So, Mr. Ryan," she said after taking a sip, "you haven't heard from your aunt or uncle?"

Shane shook his head. "If I had, I would have let you known, Detective."

"And they're not here?"

Again he shook his head.

"Is anyone else living here with you?" she asked.

"No," Shane said. "Just me and the ghosts."

She frowned. "What do you mean?"

"This place is haunted," Shane said, leaning back in his chair. "Has been since before I moved in."

She raised an eyebrow.

"Don't believe in ghosts?" Shane asked her.

"No," she answered. "No, I don't. You do?"

"Of course, I do," Shane answered. "And if you lived here, Detective, you'd believe in ghosts too."

"I'll have to take your word on it, Mr. Ryan," she said, giving him a tight smile.

A moment later, a young woman hurried into the kitchen. "Detective Lafontaine?"

"Jen?" the detective asked.

"Um, there are secret passages in the house."

The two women looked at Shane.

He put his coffee mug down and smiled at them. "Servants' passages. They run through the walls of the house. Just be careful, though. Some of them don't go where they're supposed to."

"What do you mean?" the detective asked.

"Just what I said," Shane said. "They don't go where they're supposed to. You think the passage from the pantry leads up to the floor above. You go up a few steps and suddenly there's a wall. Tomorrow, though, it might go all the way up, or it might go down into the cellar."

Detective Lafontaine looked at him with a suspicious frown, then she turned her attention back to the technician. "Check them out, and make sure you guys work in teams. It's an old house and who knows what's in the walls, or how safe they are."

"Okay, Detective," Jen said, and she left the kitchen.

Detective Lafontaine looked at him. "How long were you in the military?"

Shane knew the question was meant to catch him off guard, but it didn't.

"Twenty years," he said in French. *"When did you move to the States?"*

Her eyes widened in surprise. "When I was six. How did you know? I don't have an accent."

"You do," Shane said, hiding his satisfaction. "Only a hint of one, though. I'm a linguist, Detective. I listen to people and how they talk. It's how I knew you were born in Canada, Quebec City, if I hear it properly."

She nodded, chuckled and took a sip of her coffee. "Well done, Mr. Ryan. Well done."

He gave her a short bow.

"So," she said, settling back in her chair and crossing her legs. "Twenty years in the Marines. Did you do language work there, too?"

Shane nodded. "Later on, though. My first enlistment I was all gung ho. I went straight zero three eleven, infantry. When my captain learned about my language skills though, he browbeat me until I got a slot in the language program. Saw some combat here and there, working as an interpreter. Running and gunning when I had to."

"How many languages do you speak?" she asked.

"Speak?" Shane said. "Seventeen."

"Seventeen?" Marie asked, incredulity in her voice.

Shane nodded and smiled. "Not as difficult as you think. Languages can be grouped into families. As for myself, I read and write fluently in the romance languages, but I focus my translating work on German, French and Spanish too. Just the languages I like. With my pension from the Marines and translation jobs, I do okay."

A yell from the pantry startled them both.

Detective Lafontaine was up and out of her chair before Shane, and she opened the pantry door. An older police officer stumbled out, his eyes wide and his face pale. Once in the kitchen, he paused and blinked his eyes.

"The kitchen?" he asked.

"What's wrong, Dan?" Detective Lafontaine asked.

"The kitchen?" he repeated in a lower voice. Then he looked at the detective and said, "Marie, I was in the library."

"Okay," she said.

"Marie, the library's on the second floor. Other side away from the kitchen. I walked three steps to the right and saw another door. I went through it, and I found myself in there," he said, jerking his thumb back at the dark interior of the pantry.

Marie frowned. "You're kidding."

Dan shook his head.

The technician, Jen, hurried into the room. "Detective, Bob's missing!"

"What?" Marie asked, twisting around to face her. "What do you mean?"

"He went into a passage in a bedroom upstairs, and the door closed behind him. When we opened it, he wasn't in the passage," Jen said, her face pale.

"Why the hell did he close the door?" the detective snapped, frustrated.

"He didn't," Jen said softly. "It closed by itself."

"What room?" Shane asked, taking a step towards the technician. "What room did he go into?"

"It had a fan in it," Jen started.

"Damn it," Shane spat. "Parlor."

Without waiting for anyone he hurried out of the kitchen and heard the others follow him. He made straight for the parlor, and when he opened the door, he saw a young man. The man's hair was white, and he sat on the floor by the hearth.

"Oh my God," Jen said as she came in behind Shane. "Look at his hair."

Bob seemed to notice them for the first time, his eyes wide and unfocused. The room stank of fear.

Jen, Dan and the Detective all raced to Bob, who continued to sit numbly on the floor.

"Bob," Dan said, squatting down. "Bob."

Bob looked at Dan.

"Bob," Dan repeated. "What happened?"

"She wanted to know who I was," Bob said hoarsely. "And what I was doing in the house. In the walls. She plays in the walls."

"Who plays in the walls?" Detective Lafontaine asked gently.

"Eloise," Bob said. He looked at Shane. "She took my hand and dragged me through the floor. Straight down. The girl wants us to leave you alone."

"How old is this girl?" the detective asked.

Bob blinked. "She's eight, I think. I couldn't really tell. But, she'll never get older, Marie."

"What?" Detective Lafontaine said. "Why not?"

"Because she's dead. She said they're all dead here," Bob whispered. He pointed a trembling finger at Shane. "He's the only living one here."

Chapter 21: Forced to Wait

It was nearly eight o'clock in the evening when the police finally left, empty handed.

And Shane couldn't go into the root cellar. As much as he wanted to find information on his parents, he wanted to be alive when he did it.

If he descended into the root cellar at night, he would risk his life needlessly.

Shane would have to wait again.

The police had found nothing, however, just as the dead had promised him. He felt bad for the man named Bob, and for Dan as well. A few others had been frightened, but not to the extent of those two.

Detective Lafontaine would be back. The house had both intrigued and enraged her. She wanted to know more.

So did Shane.

He grabbed a bottle of whiskey and a tall glass out of the cabinets and carried them upstairs to the library. He turned on the light, adjusted the thermostat in the room and smiled at the loud clank the steam radiator made, as the furnace rumbled into life far below him in the basement.

Shane sat down in the large chair behind the desk, set his glass on the leather blotter and poured himself a drink. He sipped the whiskey slowly, and the liquor went down as easily as water. Soon, he would make his way to bed, make sure all the lights worked properly, and turn on the fan before he faced the nightmares again.

First, though, he told himself. *First, we'll have a little more whiskey.*

The day had been long. Terribly long. He had been able to get some work done, but only a bit. The police and their technicians had more questions than Shane had answers for when it came to the house. The police had not, of course, found the remains of his aunt and uncle. Nor had they found any traces. Not even with black lights or anything else in their bag of tricks were they able to find anything.

The dead had made sure of it.

The police had remarked on it.

Something, the police had said, should have been found. Not just evidence of his aunt and uncle, but evidence of people having lived in the house for decades. Even old blood would have shown up.

Yet not a single drop had been visible.

Detective Lafontaine told him she would be back soon, and Shane didn't doubt her.

He sighed and then he took a long drink of whiskey. Within a few minutes, he finished the glass, put it down beside the bottle and closed his eyes.

The floor creaked, and the stench of mildew and rot filled the library.

Shane opened his eyes.

It was ten past nine. He had fallen asleep.

His nostrils flared, and he realized the smell hadn't been part of a dream. The library actually stank. Shane sat up straight and looked around the room and then he froze.

On the floor by the desk were small, wet footprints. They circled the desk and then led out the library door and into the hallway.

Cautiously, Shane got to his feet and followed the trail. The tracks seemed to have started at the desk itself, as though the owner had suddenly appeared. In the hallway, the prints turned to the right, towards Shane's room. He found a large puddle just outside of his doorway, but the trail continued on to the left and did not enter.

Part of him breathed a sigh of relief as he followed the footprints farther down the hall, towards an empty front bedroom. Just before the closed door, however, the footsteps disappeared.

Shane stopped beside them and looked at the wall. A large, gilt-framed painting of a forest hung upon the wall. The piece of art was huge, perhaps four feet in width and another seven in height; the woodland scene was dark and grim; terrible things hinted within the shadows.

The canvas rippled in front of him, and a cool breeze slipped around the edges.

Shane licked his lips nervously and reached out. He had never liked the painting. In fact, he had avoided it as much as possible as a child.

Perhaps there's more to it, he told himself.

He reached out with his right hand and as he slowly traced the frame with his suspicious fingers, he immediately discovered a small protrusion. The tiniest hint of a lock he had suspected would be there.

Shane pressed it gently, and the painting swung out effortlessly into the hall.

A cold, foul wind slapped him and stung his eyes. They swelled up with tears as he took a cautious step back. He blinked them away to see what he had exposed.

Narrow stairs which led up. Straight up.

"Don't," a voice said, and Shane recognized it as the old man's. "Don't."

The voice was behind him, and Shane fought the urge to turn around, to see if he would finally catch sight of the ghost who owned the voice.

Instead, Shane managed to whisper, "Why?"

"Simply, don't," the old man said sadly. "At least not without the benefit of the sun, Shane."

Shane opened his mouth to ask why again, but closed it instead.

"Go to bed, Shane," the old man whispered. "Worry about this problem tomorrow."

Shane nodded and closed the painting over. With a nervous swallow, he went to his room and got ready for bed.

Chapter 22: Shane, October 27th, 1986

"Where did you get the picture?" his father asked.

"It was in the parlor," Shane answered. He sat on his bed and looked at his mother and father. He was confused. "Why? What's wrong with it?"

"Nothing's wrong with it, Shane," his mother said. "We just don't think your fascination with war is healthy."

Shane frowned. "I'm not fascinated with war. I like to read about history. Military history."

His father sighed. "Shane, we don't mind you reading about history. It's having a soldier's picture on your bed table. It's kind of strange. You don't even know who the man is."

"Yes, I do," Shane said.

"Really?" his mother asked skeptically. "Who is he?"

"Carl Wilhelm Hesselschwerdt," Shane answered.

His father laughed, and his mother gave him an amused smile.

"Well," she said, "you've certainly created an interesting name for him."

"I didn't," Shane said defensively.

"How do you know his name then?" his father asked between chuckles.

"He told me."

The humor vanished from his parents' faces.

"Don't be funny, Shane," his father said angrily.

"I'm not," Shane said, trying not to snap. "He told me his name. He died here."

"Did you find out about him at the library?" his mother asked, concern in her voice.

"No," Shane answered.

"Where then?" his father demanded.

"Here. He told me his name here," Shane said.

"Yes," his mother said quickly, "but, how did you know he died here?"

"Oh," Shane said. He scratched the back of his head, hesitated a moment and then he said, "Well, I found his body."

"Jesus Christ!" his father snapped, turning away and starting to pace the room.

"Where?" his mother asked and Shane could hear her trying to keep her voice calm. "Where did you find the body?"

"In the library," Shane said.

"No," his father said, turning to look at him. "You're wrong about the body. I've been in there plenty of times, Shane. There's no body."

"Yes, there is," he said angrily.

"Then show us, Shane," his mother said.

Shane got up from his bed and stomped his way out into the hallway, and into the library. He flicked on the light and went directly to the bookcase which served as a secret door. He reached in, found the switch and unlocked the case. As it popped out slightly, he took hold of the edge and pulled it the rest of the way out.

Behind him, his parents gasped in surprise, but he ignored them both. Instead, he grasped the handle of the pocket door and slid it open. Shane turned on the light and glanced down into the oubliette.

Carl's body still lay on the bottom.

Shane stepped back and gestured to the oubliette.

His mother and father moved forward and looked down. His mother turned quickly away, but his father remained and stared down. After a long moment, he too, turned away.

When both of his parents looked at him, Shane said, "It's called an oubliette; a little place of forgetting. Mr. Anderson killed him. Pushed him in and let him starve. This is the only way in or out. Carl won't tell me why he was killed."

His parents remained silent as Shane went and turned off the oubliette's light, closed the door and then the bookcase.

"We should remove the body," Shane's father said.

"No!" Shane shouted. "He doesn't want his body moved."

Both of his parents looked at him in surprise.

"We're moving the body, Shane," his father said firmly.

"And we're taking the photograph out of your room," his mother added.

The chair behind the desk was suddenly thrown into the back wall, and his parents cried out in unison.

Shane looked at them both, angry.

"Carl doesn't like what you're saying," Shane said in a low voice. "He doesn't like it at all."

Shane turned on his heel and left the library. Anger boiled in him, and he made his way to his bedroom.

Behind him, something broke in the library and his parents shrieked again in surprise.

Shane smiled angrily.

Carl wasn't happy. Not one bit.

Chapter 23: Getting a Cup of Coffee

Shane could feel something wrong in the house.

He stood in the main hallway and listened. Just below the white noise of the appliances and the neighborhood, he could hear angry murmurs.

This is not a good time to go into the root cellar. Or up the stairs behind the picture.

Anger at waiting longer to discover the fate of his parents boiled up within Shane, but he pushed it down.

Need to take a walk, he told himself. *Maybe it'll be better when I get back.*

He left the house and felt better as he made his way down the driveway. He actually smiled upon reaching the sidewalk. Shane shoved his hands in his pockets, looked up and down the street and decided to turn left towards Main Street.

He set a steady pace for himself and enjoyed the cold air on his face and in his nose. Within a few minutes, he reached Laton Street and headed to Raymond Street, where he turned again at Temple Beth Abraham and nearly bumped into Gerald and Turk.

"Shane," Gerald said happily, Turk's tail wagging as Shane patted the dog's head.

"Gerald," Shane said, shaking the man's hand. "Beautiful weather for a walk."

"It is indeed," Gerald said. "How goes it with the house?"

"Okay," Shane answered. "A little too busy yesterday; the police stopped by."

"I saw them," Gerald said.

"Evidently, my aunt and uncle got themselves lost," Shane said without much sympathy. "They left their rented car parked nearby and the police thought maybe they were in the house."

"Well," Gerald said, shaking his head. "What an unpleasant welcome to the neighborhood."

"An extremely unpleasant welcome," Shane agreed.

"What are you up to now?" Gerald asked.

"Just out for a bit of fresh air. Sometimes the house is a little too much to handle."

Gerald nodded sympathetically. "Would you like to walk back to my house? My niece should be stopping by soon."

"Trying to set me up?" Shane asked with a grin.

"No," Gerald said, laughing. "She is about your age, but, to be completely honest, I'm not sure if she even likes men."

"Fine, then," Shane said, "so long as I'm safe."

"I think you are," Gerald said, smiling.

"Lead on then, Marine," Shane said. He fell into step with Gerald, and they walked back to the older man's house. Turk trotted along easily and paused occasionally to mark a tree or bush.

Within a short time, they turned back onto Berkley Street, well past Shane's house, and made their way to Gerald's home. Parked at the curb was a large, black Dodge pickup with someone in the driver's seat.

"There she is," Gerald said with a chuckle. "She's always early. Too early, sometimes."

As they neared the truck, the driver's side door opened and Gerald's niece got out.

"Detective Lafontaine," Shane said, surprised.

She looked surprised as well, and decidedly different. She wore a pair of jeans tucked into calf-high black leather boots, and a snug gray sweater. Her hair was done nicely, and she wore a little bit of makeup.

The detective was extremely attractive.

"Marie," Gerald said, stepping forward and giving his niece a hug. "Thank you for coming over today."

"You're welcome, Uncle Gerry," she said. She squatted down and scratched Turk easily behind his ears. She looked up at Shane. "So, you know my uncle."

"I do," Shane said, nodding.

She stood up and shook her head. "I should have known. He's a busy body, and you're both Marines."

"Busy body," Gerald snorted. "Only a little bit of one."

"Come on, Uncle Gerry," she said. "Make me some of the sludge you pass off as coffee."

"Are you okay with Shane having coffee with us?" Gerald asked. "I invited him along."

"It's alright," Shane started to say.

Marie held up a hand and stopped him.

"Mr. Ryan, well, Shane, I do want to speak to you tomorrow about your aunt and uncle," she said, "but, we couldn't find a thing in your house. Do I think you did something? No. Do I think something happened to them in your house? Yes. For right now, though, let's have some coffee with my uncle before he gets too senile."

"A little too much sass from you, young lady," Gerald said, leading Turk up to the front door.

"You love it," she said, chuckling as she followed him, and Shane, in turn, followed her.

All of them went into Gerald's kitchen, and Turk laid down upon a floor mat at the back door. The dog occasionally opened an eye to make sure all was as it should be, and then he went back to sleep. Shane and Marie sat at the kitchen table, and Gerald hummed to himself as he made the coffee.

Soon the coffee maker hissed and gurgled, and Gerald took a seat.

"So, you two know each other," Gerald said.

"We do," Marie replied.

"Officially," Gerald said.

She and Shane both nodded.

"Alright then, let's introduce you two unofficially. Shane, this is my niece Marie Lafontaine, a detective with the Nashua Police Department," Gerald said. "Marie, this is Shane Ryan. He's my neighbor, and he works as a translator."

"There," Gerald said with a grin, "you two are introduced."

"A pleasure," Shane said honestly, and he extended his hand over the table. Marie gave a curt nod, shook his hand warmly and offered a small smile.

"Now this isn't about work," Marie said, "but I have to ask, were you serious about your house being haunted?"

"Of course," Shane said.

Marie looked doubtfully at him.

"Don't discount it, Marie," Gerald said gently. He stood up and went to the cabinet above the coffee maker. He took down a trio of blue ceramic mugs. As he filled each one, he continued. "The house is haunted. Has been haunted for as long as I've lived here."

"Uncle Gerry," Marie said, laughing. "There's no such thing as ghosts. Even the stuff we saw yesterday can be chalked up to fear and confusion."

Gerald brought the coffee to the table, set a mug down in front of each of them and then sat once more. After a moment of silence, Gerald asked, "Marie, did you listen to the house when you got there yesterday?"

"No," Marie said, smiling. "I didn't *listen* to the house."

"What about the yard?" Gerald asked.

She shook her head. "Why?"

"I ask because if you had, you wouldn't have heard anything," Gerald said.

"Am I supposed to?" she asked, frowning.

"Listen now," Gerald said.

Shane listened as quiet settled over them. Beyond the windows and door, he heard birds. They called out loudly for spring, and their songs filled the air. He could even hear a squirrel yell.

"What?" Marie asked. "What am I supposed to be listening to?"

"You hear the animals?" Gerald asked. "The birds and the squirrels?"

"Yes," she said, a tinge of anger creeping into her tone. "Of course, I do."

"You won't at Shane's house," Gerald said. He took a drink of his coffee. "You won't hear any birds there. Nor any squirrels."

Marie laughed and shook her head. "You're crazy, Uncle Gerry."

Her voice trailed off though as she realized he was serious.

"Come off it," she said, frowning. "You can't be serious."

She looked from her uncle to Shane, and Shane nodded. She picked up her mug, took a sip, and then she said, "Why?"

Gerald looked at Shane and waited.

"The house is haunted," Shane said. "It has been since I moved in, and, from what I've read, it was haunted long before me, too."

"Who haunts it?" Marie asked. Her tone of disbelief had been replaced by a more professional curiosity.

"Not one, but many," Shane said.

"You told me you lived alone," Marie said. "Tell me, who's the young man I saw the day before yesterday?"

"Upstairs window?" Shane asked.

She nodded.

"Probably Carl," Shane said.

"And how long has he lived with you?" Marie asked.

Shane smiled. "Carl's dead, Marie. He's a ghost. He's been there for a very long time."

"Did you see him in the upper right window?" Gerald asked.

"Yes," Marie answered.

"I saw him for the first time in nineteen sixty-eight, when your aunt and I were looking at this house," Gerald said softly. "Mr. Hall, who lived across from me, said he had been seeing Carl since the early forties."

Marie looked from her uncle to Shane and shook her head. "I really can't believe this."

Shane shrugged. "If you like, come home with me after coffee."

She raised an eyebrow.

"Sorry," Shane said, chuckling, "definitely came out wrong. If you'd like to visit after coffee, we'll see if Carl, or any of them, are up for company."

"Fair enough," Marie said. She drank some of her coffee and grimaced. "Jesus, Uncle Gerry, did you drain your oil tank and run it through the coffee maker?"

"Just for you," Gerald said with a chuckle. "Just for you."

Chapter 24: Shane, September 19th, 1987

"Are you sure you're going to be okay?" Shane's mother asked him for the fourth time.

He managed to not roll his eyes as he nodded. "Yes, mom."

His father adjusted his tie as he looked over at him.

"We're just worried about you in this house alone," his father said. "Well, at night at least."

Shane glanced out the front sitting room's window at the treetops lit by the sun as it slowly set. He looked back to his parents and smiled. "I'll be okay."

His mother gave him a worried smile, and his father said, "Alright, kid. No girls, though, okay?"

Shane shook his head, and his mother slapped his father's arm, and not playfully.

"Enough, Hank," she said. She looked at Shane. "Listen, you have the number for the Hunt Building. Call it if you have any trouble. Or go over to Mrs. Kensington's house."

Shane nodded.

He wouldn't have any trouble. At least not until he slept. The dark ones, the ghosts in the root cellar, were the only ones who bothered him now. They slipped in when his parents were asleep. When the other ghosts were lost in their own memories.

But I'm supposed to talk with Carl, tonight, Shane reminded himself. They would work on practicing Shane's German.

"I'll be okay," Shane said. He smiled. He knew he would be okay, but he couldn't explain it to his parents. If they knew he was going to spend most of the night in a conversation with Carl, whose picture his mother constantly hid, they wouldn't be happy.

"Alright," his mother said with a sigh. She gave him a quick kiss, wiped off the faint trace of lipstick it left behind from his forehead, and then she hugged him tightly. "Alright."

His father gave him a pat on the head and then Shane watched them leave. The limousine was at the front door and in a moment, the large black car pulled away with his parents inside.

With his parents gone, Shane left the parlor and went upstairs to the library. He found a copy of *Sturm* by Ernst Junger, and he sat down in the chair with it. Patiently, he looked at the words and carefully translated each sentence in his mind. Line by line, paragraph by paragraph. He worked his way through the first page, and then the second.

His eyes grew tired, and he stifled a yawn as he tried to stay awake.

He was always tired.

He never felt as though he had rested.

The dead were too noisy.

The light went out, and the door clicked shut.

Shane heard the lock turn.

His hands started to sweat, and he put the book down on the desk. His heart threatened to beat its way out of his chest, but Shane forced himself to breathe. He needed to be in control.

Something or someone would be in the room soon, and it wouldn't be Carl.

He could *feel* the difference in the air.

"Shane," a female voice said. "Shane Ryan."

It wasn't Eloise. A hint of darkness stained the voice and filled him with fear.

"Shane," the female said again, dragging his name out in the darkness.

He realized the room was completely black. He couldn't see anything. He felt as though he had been thrust into a box and the lid slammed shut.

The oubliette, Shane thought. *This is what it would feel like to be in the oubliette, with no way out.*

"Who are you?" Shane whispered.

"Vivienne, or Nimue," the female said, laughing easily, frighteningly. "You should read *Le Morte D'Arthur*, Shane. I draw my name as easily as he drew the sword."

Shane had read *The Death of Arthur*. "You're not the lady in the lake."

Vivienne snorted in disgust. "What do you know? You're still clinging to your meat. Come to the pond, Shane. Come down and swim with the ducks."

"You don't like ducks," he answered.

"I hate them!" she spat, and Shane reeled back in surprise and horror. A stench had suddenly enveloped him. The odor choked him, and he nearly threw up as he pushed himself back away from the desk.

He wanted to jump out of the chair, but he knew he couldn't.

The room was too dark.

She was in the room, and who knew how much bigger the room could get. The house followed no rules.

Shane could literally become lost in the library.

"You'll visit me soon," Vivienne whispered, her voice suddenly close to his ear. "Yes, you will, Shane. You'll have no choice. You will visit me soon."

The light in the room flared into life, and he turned away. He rubbed at his eyes and a moment later he was able to see again.

Shane was still in the chair, but it was by the door instead of behind the desk.

Wet footprints dried slowly on the hardwood floor.

Shane took a deep breath and wondered if he could make it to the relative safety of his bedroom.

Chapter 25: Introductions are Made

Shane had barely finished his morning medicinal shot of whiskey when the doorbell rang.

Jesus Christ, he thought. He put the glass on the bed table and hurried down the stairs. *Who the hell is here this early?*

Shane needed to get into the root cellar.

He needed to look for his parents.

It can't be Detective Lafontaine, he thought as he reached the door. *Six thirty is way too early.*

Detective Marie Lafontaine stood at the doorstep dressed in her 'civilian' clothes. Once more Shane was impressed with just how attractive the woman was.

"Shane," she said, nodding her head. "Is this too early?"

"No," Shane said, stepping aside to let her in. "I'm just surprised."

"Well," she said as he closed the door, "I drink coffee pretty early in the morning."

Shane looked over at her and saw her smile.

He chuckled, shook his head and said, "Yeah. I didn't think about the time."

"So," she said, looking around. "Since I'm not here on official business, are you going to introduce me?"

"Yes," Shane said.

Marie looked at him. "Did you have a drink?"

"I have a drink every morning," Shane said. "And every night."

"You might have a problem, Shane," she said. There was no condemnation in her voice, no tone of judgment.

"I do have a problem," he said tiredly. "I grew up here. This house is a nightmare, with brief moments of respite."

"Then why did you come back?" she asked.

"I need to know what happened to my parents," he answered.

Marie frowned. "What do you mean?"

"Your uncle didn't tell you?" Shane asked.

She shook her head. "He plays things close to the vest."

"Fair enough. Follow me into the kitchen," he said. "I'll tell you in there. Have you had breakfast?"

"Yes," she said.

He led her in, pulled out a chair and fixed his toast, coffee, oatmeal, and his water. "Coffee?"

"Please," Marie said. "Yours is a lot better than Uncle Gerry's."

"Thanks," Shane said, chuckling.

"When did your parents disappear?" she asked after he had gotten everything ready and sat down across from her.

"When I graduated from boot camp, basic training down on Parris Island," Shane said. "They were supposed to see me graduate. They never showed up. My father didn't go to work for a few days, and his boss got nervous. My dad never missed work. Not if he could help it. The police came, checked out the house, found it unlocked. But, no sign of my parents, though. It's been almost twenty-five years."

"Did you ever find out what happened?" Marie asked.

Shane shook his head. "It's the only reason why I'm back here. Some of the dead are alright, like Carl."

"Carl?" she asked.

"He's probably the young man you saw in the window," Shane said. "He shifts his form from young to old and back again. I don't think it's intentional. Anyway, I was going to start looking for my parents this morning. I didn't expect you to be here quite so early."

"Shane," Marie said, looking at him with concern. "We went through the house the other day. We didn't find anything or anyone. And we're experts at finding stuff."

"They're still here," Shane said softly. He drank some of his coffee, and he gave her a small, tired smile. "I doubt they're still alive, but they're still here."

Marie looked at him for a moment and then she asked, "Where do you think they are?"

"I don't know. I know where they went in, and so I can only follow," he answered.

"What do you mean?" Marie asked. "Went into where?"

"Into the house," Shane said.

"They were already in the house when they disappeared, right?" she asked.

"Yes, but you can disappear into the walls. Places and rooms which shouldn't exist, but they do anyway." Shane finished his coffee.

"You're not making any sense, Shane," she said.

"*She doesn't seem to know anything,*" Carl said from behind Shane.

Marie stiffened, her cup shook in her hand and splashed coffee onto the table.

"*Not about this, no,*" Shane answered.

Carl's voice moved from behind Shane, his next words spoken from near the sink. "*Do you wish for her to see me? She shall, perhaps, understand you a little better?*"

"Are you throwing your voice?" Marie asked, looking at him with a confused expression.

"No," Shane answered. "I'm not."

Carl suddenly appeared, the edges of his body hazy, as though viewed through a camera with a scratched lens.

Marie's eyes widened with fear, and the coffee mug fell from her hands and struck the table loudly.

Chapter 26: Shane, December 31st, 1988

Shane was home alone, his parents now comfortable with the idea. It didn't bother Shane too much. It was better to be awake in the house than to be asleep. Occasionally the dead startled him, but being awake when it happened was much easier to handle. When Thaddeus or Eloise slipped into his room and whispered in his ears, the initial fear was terrible.

With his parents at Mrs. Kensington's New Year's Eve party, Shane was free to do what he wanted. Within reason of course.

Shane knew his limits. An entire pack of Oreo cookies and a gallon of milk was unacceptable for a snack. Perhaps he could get away with half of each. He was hungry.

He whistled as he took a handful of cookies out of the package and then went to the fridge. Shane took out the gallon, stood there with the refrigerator door open and drank long and deep. When he finished, he wiped his mouth with the sleeve of his sweatshirt, returned the milk to its proper place in the fridge, and closed the door.

With a satisfied belch, Shane left the kitchen and popped an entire Oreo into his mouth. He made his way to the second floor and headed towards the library.

From the third floor, he heard the groan of old hinges.

Shane stopped and listened.

The noise sounded again and slowly shifted into a long, drawn out squeal.

He had been to the third floor only a few times but he had never stayed long. The temperature up there was always colder, the walls barren of decoration. None of the lights worked, even though an electrician hired by Shane's father said they should. The doors in the hall were always locked, too.

They were *always* locked.

Shane walked to the small, hidden door at the end of the hall. He opened it and took a step back. The lights were on in the stairwell.

He stood in the doorway long enough to finish his cookies. Shane brushed his hands off on his jeans and then he climbed the stairs. Another door stood at the top, he opened it and stepped into the third-floor hallway.

Light spilled out of every wall sconce. Out of the four doors in the hallway, the last one on the left was open. Not a little, or only slightly. Not half, but fully open and against the wall.

Shane heard music.

A violin.

The music drifted out of the open doorway and slipped down the hall. Each note followed the other gliding off the bare plaster and along the worn wooden floor.

Shane approached the open door carefully. The music gradually grew louder and soon he was only a step away. For a moment, he paused, took a deep breath, and moved forward to look in.

Shane blinked and shook his head.

A set of stairs stretched up in front of him. They led to a fourth floor, but there wasn't a fourth floor. At least not when you looked at the house from the outside.

The strange stairwell was dim, and Shane could barely see a door at the top. The sound of the violin came through it and rolled out and around him.

Shane took a moment to build up his courage, and then walked up the stairs.

The music increased in both tempo and volume.

The unseen musician seemed to sense his approach.

Shane paused for a moment, and so too did the music. The last note hung in the air and lingered.

Shane, in spite of the trepidation he felt, smiled and continued up the stairs.

The music started up again.

The door at the top of the stairs was tall and narrow, barely wide enough for Shane to pass through if it was unlocked. He reached out and took hold of the cut crystal doorknob, found it warm and the edges smooth, as he carefully turned it.

The latch clicked loudly, and the door swung into the unknown room.

The music washed over Shane as he stepped into a dimly lit space. Thick rugs covered the floor, and stacks of written music were piled around the room haphazardly. The room, like the door, was tall and narrow. It was also long and barren of windows. On the wood-paneled walls, dozens of violins and their bows rested on individual shelves.

The end of the room was hidden in a shadow behind a solitary floor lamp. The music came from the darkness; a pure, beautiful sound. Shane's heart ached with each note.

He cautiously walked forward, and the music stopped.

"I'm sorry," Shane said softly. "I don't mean to interrupt."

"*You're not interrupting, Child,*" a man said. The language wasn't German, or French, but something else. Similar to French, but not the same.

"*Will you continue to play?*" Shane asked, and he couldn't keep the surprise out of his voice as he heard himself speak the man's language.

"*Of course, I will,*" the man chuckled. "*I had heard of your ability to speak, but I did not know it would include my own.*"

"*What am I speaking?*" Shane asked.

"*Italian, Child,*" he said.

"*Are you dead?*" Shane asked as politely as he could.

The man laughed. "*Yes. I am dead. Long dead, I am afraid.*"

"*May I ask your name?*"

"*You may, and I will even tell you. Roberto Guidoboni.*"

"*Why are you here?*" Shane asked.

"*My music,*" Roberto said. A beautiful note escaped the shadow. "*I feared I would not be able to make my music after my death, and so I built myself this room. I put my violins in it, and when I was sure death was near, I locked myself in.*"

"*But,*" Shane hesitated, then he continued on. "*But, this room doesn't exist. It shouldn't even be part of the house.*"

Roberto laughed. "*Well, it did exist. It was a secret room in my house, yet it burned. Later, when Anderson purchased my home, my room remained, and the new house kept me here. She lets me play. When it suits her.*"

"*The one in the pond?*" Shane whispered.

"*Yes,*" he answered. "*The one in the pond.*"

"*Will you... will you still play?*" Shane asked, hopeful.

"*I will. You are not afraid of the dead?*"

"*Not all of the dead,*" he said.

Roberto chuckled. *"Well said, Child. Well said. Would you look upon me as I play?"*

"Yes," Shane answered.

"Excellent."

The light shifted slightly, and suddenly Shane could see Roberto Guidoboni.

A skeleton clad in rags.

He sat on a high stool, the tattered remains of house slippers on the bones of his feet. He tucked a violin under his chin, somehow worked his fingers around the neck of the instrument to place them on the strings, and carefully drew the bow back in one long, graceful motion.

Shane sighed and sat down on the floor. He closed his eyes and listened to the music the dead man created.

Chapter 27: The Root Cellar

"Marie," Shane said gently. "Marie, are you alright?"

She turned her attention away from Carl and stared at Shane. She blinked several times and then she asked, "Is this real?"

Shane nodded.

"How?" she said, looking over at Carl and then back to Shane. "How can this possibly be real? There are no such things as ghosts."

"Will she be well?" Carl asked.

"Yes," Shane said. *"I think so."*

"What are you speaking?" Marie asked. "Is it German?"

"Yes," Shane said.

Marie looked at him, shook her head and said, "This is real."

It wasn't a question.

"Yes," Shane said.

"Okay," she said. The muscles of her jaw tightened and relaxed several times before she nodded. "Okay. Does he speak English?"

"He does," Shane answered.

"Will he?" She asked.

"No," Shane said, trying not to smile.

Marie frowned. "Why not?"

"He doesn't like to," Shane said.

"Well," she said, "does he know where your parents went?"

"No," Shane said. "Just where they went in."

"And where did they go in?" she asked.

"The root cellar."

Marie stood up. "It's in the pantry, right?"

"Yes," Shane answered, standing up as well. He walked to the pantry and opened the door. He turned on the light and pointed to the trapdoor which led down. "I need to go down there."

"Let's go," she said.

"What?" he asked.

"Let's go," she repeated. "I need to see what's down there."

"Tell her it isn't safe," Carl said, stepping towards them.

"It's not safe," Shane said. "Not at all."

"I know," Marie said, smiling tightly. "I figured it wouldn't be. Will your friend be coming with us?"

"No," Shane answered. "It's not safe for him down there."

"He's afraid?" Marie asked, surprised.

"Yes," Shane said. "Just because he's dead doesn't mean he wants to vanish from the world. Are you sure you want to go down there with me?"

"Absolutely sure," she said.

"Okay," Shane said. He walked into the pantry, bent down and pulled up the trap door.

A terrible wave of cold air rushed out of the darkness, and Shane staggered back. He and Marie coughed and wheezed at the stench of old death heavy in the air.

"Jesus Christ," Marie hissed. "It didn't smell like this yesterday when we opened it."

"I don't remember it ever smelling like this," Shane said. "Or it being this cold either."

He took a small LED flashlight off a shelf, turned it on and pointed it down the ladder. The darkness tried to eat away at the cone of light, which revealed a hard-packed dirt floor. Shane looked over at Marie.

"Ready?" he asked her.

"Yes," Marie said, nodding. She slipped a hand into her pocket and took out her own flashlight. Marie grinned at him. "Better than a boy scout."

Shane smiled. "Yes, you are."

He looked back down the ladder, ignored the nervous rumble of his stomach, and descended into the root cellar. When he reached the bottom, he pointed the flashlight at each of the walls. They were made of large, rough cut stones with small niches carved in them. In the far left corner, a stone had been removed, and blackness awaited.

Marie reached the floor and a moment later, her flashlight's beam joined his.

"There?" she asked him.

"Yes," Shane said with a nod. He walked forward, and Marie was barely a step behind him. Finally, just a few steps away from the darkness, the light cut through it. A small, oval doorway was revealed, absent of any door, though. The floor beyond was made of smooth stone, and it gently sloped down.

The walls and ceiling were of the same type of stone and the passage turned slightly to the right. Within a few feet, the remainder of it was hidden. The foul smell and cold air of the room emanated from the tunnel.

"This wasn't here," Marie said.

"No," Shane said in agreement. "It wasn't. I've never seen it before, and I thought I had seen just about everything this house had hidden."

Something splashed in the distance, and Shane stiffened.

"What is it?" Marie asked. "What's wrong?"

"Did you hear the splash?"

"Yes," she said. "Is it bad?"

"More than likely," Shane said softly.

"Well," Marie said, taking a deep breath, "only one way to find out."

Shane nodded and stepped into the tunnel.

Instantly it felt as though the walls would close in on him and he had to crouch slightly or else he would hit his head on the ceiling. He reached a hand out to steady himself and pulled it back quickly.

"What's wrong?" Marie asked.

"The wall," Shane answered. "It felt wrong."

"Oh Jesus," she said after a moment. "Feels like mucus."

"Yeah," he said. He continued forward. He followed the path of his own flashlight as the passage curved. And it continued to curve and descend in a tight circle.

"I hope we don't have to come back up this way," Marie said after a minute.

"Why not?" Shane asked.

"I'm having a hard time not slipping right now," she answered. "Can you imagine what it'll be like going up this path?"

"No," Shane said. "I can't."

After a long time, the floor leveled out and the passage straightened. Slowly, it widened as well. The walls disappeared, and only the floor remained. No matter where they pointed the flashlights, they only found darkness and the stones upon which they walked.

"Shane," Marie said after a few minutes of walking.

"Yes?" he asked.

"Is there something up ahead?" she asked.

Shane moved the beam of his flashlight towards hers, and he saw a small shape on the floor. He hurried forward and came to a sharp stop.

"It's a belt," Marie said. She stepped past Shane and squatted down.

A long, dark brown, leather belt lay curled on the stones. The silver buckle was face down. She reached out to turn it over with her flashlight.

But Shane already knew what the buckle had engraved on it.

"'H R,'" Marie said, looking up at him.

"Henry Ryan," Shane said. "Well, he preferred Hank."

"Your dad's?" Marie asked.

Shane nodded. "Yes. I gave him the belt on his birthday when I was fourteen."

"Why is it here?" she asked, looking at him.

"He loved to wear it," Shane said sadly. "He wore it all the time. He said a man always needed to wear a belt or suspenders. And he hated suspenders. He always had it on."

Reverently, Marie picked up the belt and handed it to Shane.

"Thank you," Shane said softly. He took the belt, wrapped it into a tight loop and slipped it into his back pocket.

Marie stood up and looked around the darkness. "Well, which way from here?"

Her flashlight flickered and went out.

"Take my hand," Shane said quickly, extending his free hand to her.

Marie clasped it just as his own flashlight was extinguished.

Over the sound of his own heartbeat, Shane heard the slap of something wet against stone.

It was repeated, rhythmically.

"Something's walking," Marie said.

He tightened his grip on her and fought down a wave of fear.

"Do not let go," he whispered. "No matter what you do. Do not let go."

The walker drew closer.

"What is it?" Marie asked in a low voice.

"I think it's the girl in the pond," he said softly, unable to keep a quiver of terror out of his voice. "We need to leave."

The darkness pressed down upon them, and Marie asked, "How?"

Before Shane could answer he caught a bit of music.

A violin playing part of Schubert's *Death and the Maiden*.

Shane turned towards the sound. It grew louder, if only slightly. "Do you hear it?"

"Hear... wait, is someone playing a violin?" Marie asked.

"Yes," Shane said excitedly. "We need to get to it."

"Let's go, then," Marie said, as she led the way towards the instrument.

They moved at a steady pace. The music became louder, and so did the sound of the walker. The force's pace quickened as they drew closer to the musician.

Suddenly, a thin, horizontal line of light appeared in the darkness ahead of them.

"Run!" Shane hissed.

The two of them ran for the light, which grew faintly larger and revealed the bottom of a wooden door.

The walker ran.

Shane slammed into the door, found the cut crystal knob and twisted it violently. The lock clicked, as they stumbled in. Light blinded him, and he rolled across a carpeted floor. The music stopped, and Shane shouted, "The door!"

The door slammed shut, and he panted as he lay on the floor.

Chapter 28: With the Musician

Marie rested her head against the cool wood of the door and her hands on plush carpets. She slowly got herself under control, opened her eyes and looked down.

Water seeped beneath the door and into the fabric of the carpets.

Marie stared at it for a moment, confused, until something heavy hit the door. She pushed herself backward and bumped into Shane. They both stared at the door.

She could worry about the room they were in later.

The real threat was on the other side of the wooden door.

The walker, for who else could it be, knocked.

A voice from behind Marie, and it wasn't Shane's, said something in what sounded like Italian.

Another knock was the only response.

The tone of the speaker changed from courteous to angry. The Italian was spoken quickly.

The door shuddered in its frame. Once. Twice. Three times.

And then Marie could hear the presence leave. The slap of the feet grew fainter.

Shane stood up and said, "Marie, I'd like to introduce you to our host. Roberto Guidoboni."

She turned and froze, horrified.

Roberto Guidoboni was dead. A skeleton clad in rags as he held a violin. He bestowed upon her a death's head grin and spoke to her in soft, delicate Italian.

Marie stood shocked, not quite sure what to say.

Stunned, she let Shane guide her to an ancient armchair. He murmured for her to sit down, and she did, unable to take her eyes off of the skeleton, though. Shane sat down on the floor beside her and spoke in Italian to Roberto.

The skeleton bowed his head and placed his violin between his shoulder and his chin. His fleshless fingers danced across the neck and the bow flew along the strings.

A deep, beautiful rhythm filled the room, and Marie shook as her adrenaline high crashed.

Chapter 29: Shane, January 20th, 1989

Shane hurried through the snow, but he wasn't going to make it.

Keith and Matthew were too close. He could hear Christopher, larger and slower, laugh as Shane tried to get home.

Shane passed his wall and made it to his driveway.

He needed his front door, though. The steps at least.

Halfway to safety, Keith's hand landed on Shane's shoulder. The older boy grabbed Shane's parka and jerked him backward. Shane grunted as he landed hard on his backside. He scrambled to his feet and found the other three boys in front of him. Keith stood in the middle, the tallest of the three and the leanest. Matthew was slightly thicker and a little shorter. Christopher, red-faced from the race through the snow, was the shortest and the widest.

And Shane stood alone in the driveway against them.

His mother was gone, at least until four.

She had a dentist appointment.

His father was still at work.

Shane was alone.

"Why'd you run, freak?" Keith asked, sneering.

"Leave me alone, Keith," Shane said. He hated the sound of fear in his own voice, but he knew the three boys wanted to beat him up. There was no one to stop them.

Shane would fight, and he would lose.

"Leave me alone, Keith," Matthew said, pitching his voice high and mimicking Shane. Keith and Christopher laughed.

Keith took off his gloves and dropped them into the snow.

"I like the way it feels on my knuckles," Keith explained. "You know, when the blood hits them."

Shane shrugged off his backpack and held a strap tightly in his right hand. His heart beat quickly. All three of the other boys were bigger and older than Shane. They had picked on him ever since he started middle school.

They always seemed to know when neither of his parents were home.

Keith cracked his knuckles and grinned.

"Hit him!" Christopher said excitedly. "Hit him, Keith!"

"I will," Keith said happily, raising his fist as he stepped forward.

A loud groan spilled out from the house and washed over them.

They all froze.

"What the hell just happened?" Matthew asked, looking around.

Shane looked around nervously. The house seemed to have darkened. A shadow had slipped over it. Some of the trees bent in different directions.

"You need to leave," Shane whispered. "Something bad is going to happen."

Christopher laughed. "Yeah, Keith's going to beat you up."

"Knock it off," Keith said sharply, lowering his hand. "Something's wrong."

"You need to go," Shane said, desperately. All of the trees were moving now. "*Please,* you need to leave."

A whisper, indistinct, raced across the snow. A shadow slipped into the driveway and stopped in the center. It blocked the way to the street. The way to safety.

"We need to get inside," Shane said in a low voice.

"What?" Matthew asked, surprised.

"All of us need to get inside now," Shane said. "We have to go in."

"Why would we go in with you?" Christopher said, grinning. "You want a beating inside your own house?"

Keith saw the shadow in the driveway. The shadow over the house. The way the trees moved. The bully looked at Shane.

"Can we?" Keith asked in a low voice.

Shane nodded. "Just run. The door's open."

Keith turned and ran for the door, and Shane followed him. Matthew followed and with a snort of disgust, Christopher did too.

Keith reached the door, opened it and led the way into the house. A moment later, Shane and the others piled in.

Shane closed the door, and something outside screamed.

"Holy Jesus!" Christopher said, stumbling backward and crossing himself.

"Lock the door," Matthew said nervously.

"It won't matter," Shane said, feeling better as he took off his backpack. "Not if it really wants to come in. It usually doesn't though, and if it does, it doesn't like what happens."

"What happens?" Keith asked.

"Carl happens," Shane answered. He removed his jacket, opened the hall closet and hung it up. He took off his boots and put them on the boot tray by the door. When he was done, he looked at the three boys. They had wanted to hurt him a few minutes earlier, but *it* had come. The thing in the yard. The thing he hated.

These were just boys. Stupid boys.

And Shane wasn't mad at them.

"Do you guys want something to eat?" He asked.

The three of them looked at him in surprise. After a moment, Keith nodded.

"Okay," Shane said. "Just take your boots and jackets off. You can call your moms in the kitchen."

He waited as they shed their backpacks and winter gear. Soon all of them stood in their school uniforms and stockings.

"Come on," Shane said. He passed through them and led the way to the kitchen. Upstairs, a door slammed, opened, and then it slammed again.

"Is your mom home?" Matthew asked.

"No," Shane said. "No one's home but me."

"What?" Christopher asked. "Who made that noise then? Who banged the door?"

"Probably the old man," Shane said, gesturing to the kitchen table. "Sit down."

"What old man? Your dad?" Keith asked.

Shane shook his head. "No. The old man. The old ghost. He spends a lot of time upstairs. He's a real pain. All he does is complain."

Keith and Matthew looked nervously up at the ceiling towards the second floor, but Christopher laughed.

"You're full of it, Shane," the boy sneered.

"Shut up, Chris," Keith snapped.

96

Christopher looked at him in surprise.

"So," Keith said, looking at Shane, "this place is really haunted?"

Shane nodded.

"Bad?" Matthew asked.

"Yeah," Shane said, taking down four short glasses. "Bad. I have to sleep with the lights on and the door off of the hinges."

"You're a liar," Christopher said angrily. "There's no such thing as ghosts."

The back door rattled.

Shane looked at him and for the first time realized he didn't have to be afraid of the older boy. Of any of them.

"Do you want milk or water?" He asked.

"Milk," Keith and Matthew said.

"You need to tell me how you're doing this," Christopher said, his face going red. "You need to tell me."

"Knock it off!" Keith yelled.

"No," Christopher said, his voice getting higher. "No! There's no such thing as ghosts!"

All of the windows darkened, as though someone had painted each pane black.

"There are," Shane said softly. "And there are a lot here."

"How many?" Matthew whispered.

"At least six, maybe more," Shane answered. "And yes, they can hurt you."

Christopher opened his mouth to speak and then he stopped. His eyes widened in surprise, and his blonde hair stood straight up. He got up from his chair, and Shane realized someone had the boy by the hair.

Christopher started to cry, and he wet his pants.

"Carl," Shane said, and he hoped it was the dead German. *"Please let him go."*

"Fine," Carl said, and Christopher sat down hard in his chair, the wood creaking beneath his weight.

Keith and Matthew looked in horror at their friend.

"Carl doesn't like bullies," Shane explained. "And he doesn't like people who make too much noise."

When none of the three boys responded to the statement, Shane walked to the pantry, opened it and asked, "Do you guys want Oreos?"

Chapter 30: A Glass of Wine

Shane poured the red wine into a glass and handed it to Marie, who accepted it gratefully. Her hands shook slightly and for a minute, he was worried he might have to help her hold the glass steady enough to drink from.

But, she managed.

"She will be fine," Roberto said, playing a small piece on his violin. *"I can tell."*

"Yes, I think so," Shane agreed.

Marie looked from Shane to the skeleton and back to Shane.

Well, Shane thought. *I hope she'll be alright.*

"How are you holding up, Marie?" he asked her.

"Okay," she said. She took a long drink from the wine glass and looked at him. "This is all real."

"Yes," Shane said.

"And your parents disappeared down here twenty odd years ago?" she asked.

"Yes."

She frowned and after a moment she said, "Can I see the belt?"

"The belt?" he asked, and then he remembered. "Oh, yes."

He reached into his back pocket and pulled it out.

She took it from him and examined it. "Shane, this hasn't been down here for twenty years. Hell, I don't think it's been down here for more than a few weeks."

"What?" he asked, squatting down beside her.

"Look," she said, "the leather should be rotted, and the belt buckle should be covered in muck."

"That is your father's belt, is it not?" Roberto asked.

Shane looked over at him and nodded. *"How do you know?"*

"He was wearing it when I saw him," the dead man answered.

Shane straightened up. *"What? When did you see him?"*

"I am not sure," Roberto said apologetically. *"Time is...it is not as I remember it. Nothing is."*

"When do you think you saw him last?" Shane asked, trying to fight down his hope, knowing it to be futile.

"A week ago. Perhaps two," he answered.

"What did he say?" Marie asked. "Does he know something?"

Shane nodded. "He says he thinks he saw my father a week or two ago. *Roberto, was my mother with him?"*

"No, Shane, I am sorry to say. I have not seen her in quite some time. He is searching for her. But the girl, she keeps them apart."

Shane passed the information on to Marie. She finished her wine and stood up.

"Ask him where your father was headed," she said.

Shane did so, and he translated Roberto's response. "Into the attic."

"Can we get there?" She asked.

"It depends on which one," Shane said. "There are several, from what Carl has told me."

Outside of the door came the sudden sound of wet feet on stone.

"Quickly," Roberto said. *"You must leave, Shane."*

Shane turned to the door he had entered when he was only a boy. *"Thank you, my friend."*

Roberto nodded.

"Come on, Marie," Shane said. "We need to leave."

He led the way out. Narrow stairs led down to the next floor. With Marie close behind him, he hurried down to the hallway at the bottom. Behind them, someone banged on the door to the stone room.

Roberto yelled in Italian at the stranger.

Shane reached the hall and waited for Marie.

"Where the hell are we?" She asked, looking around. "I don't recognize this place."

"The servants' quarters," Shane said.

"These weren't here yesterday," Marie said as they headed to the exit which would lead them to the second floor.

"I know," Shane said. "A lot of things weren't. They might not be here tomorrow."

Shane opened the far door and led Marie down the next flight of stairs.

"Are we on the second floor now?" Marie asked.

"Yes," Shane said.

"How?" she said, turning around to look at him. "How is it even possible?"

"What do you mean?" he asked.

"We never went up, Shane," Marie said. "Never. We went down. And down. And *down*. We even came down out of the damn musical skeleton room. We never went *up*."

"No. We didn't."

"Then it's not possible," Marie said angrily.

"Everything's impossible until it isn't," Shane said, shrugging his shoulders. Downstairs, the grandfather clock struck the hour.

Noon, he thought. His stomach rumbled in agreement.

"So, Detective Lafontaine," Shane said. "Do you feel like having lunch?"

Chapter 31: Shane, February 10th, 1988

Shane put the phone back in its cradle and for the first time in a long time, he looked at himself and realized he was afraid.

His parents weren't going to be home. The car had broken down in Connecticut, and they couldn't even find a car to rent.

Shane was going to be alone in the house, overnight.

They had called around to the neighbors, but no one had answered.

He felt panic well within him but he tried to ignore it.

Then again there wasn't any place safe. Not at night.

He started to sweat, and he left the parlor. Shane quickly went upstairs and went into the library. He turned the light on and went to sit in the leather armchair behind the desk.

The house was silent.

Shane couldn't hear anything. Not the old man, not the violinist. Not Thaddeus and not Eloise. Even Carl was absent.

The house didn't settle, and the air was cold. He couldn't hear the furnace or the wind which bent the tops of the trees in the pale light cast by the February moon.

The silence terrified him.

Shane swallowed nervously, got up from the chair and walked to a window. He looked down on the back yard. In the center of the pond, beneath the ice, he knew the dead girl waited. She wanted him, and he didn't know why.

It doesn't matter why, he told himself. *You just can't let her get you. You can't.*

As he stood in the window, something moved and caught his eye.

Someone walked into the yard from Chester Street. It was a man, from what Shane could see. He carried a backpack and was dressed in warm clothes. His winter coat was blue, and so was the knit cap he wore. It looked like he had on black pants and work boots.

And suddenly the man changed direction. He walked towards the house instead of away from it.

Is he going to try and break in? Shane wondered. *Can't he feel how wrong the house is?*

The man stepped closer to the house, out of Shane's sight.

With a sigh, Shane returned to the desk and the chair.

Something scratched in the walls.

The noise became louder, and soon it sounded as if dozens of people ran through the servants' passages. Within a moment, silence returned.

A scream raced through the house and exploded out of the iron heating vents set in the library's floor. The scream ended abruptly, and laughter followed.

Shane sat stiffly in the chair while he listened.

The sound of footsteps returned, this time in the hallway.

Shane looked out the open door and waited. Soon the feet drew closer, laughter echoed off the walls, and something heavy was dragged along the floor.

The first shape that Shane saw, was nothing more than a shadow. Dark, far too dark for the hall. It crept into the doorway and was only two or three feet high. The vague semblance of a head turned towards him. Eyes the color of an electric blue spark looked at him, and then the head turned away. The shadowy creature moved forward and passed beyond the doorway.

Others followed, though, and they carried the man who Shane had seen in the back yard.

He was stripped naked and his limbs were bound together in rusted wire. When his head appeared Shane stifled a scream as he saw the man's wild, terrified eyes. A black shadow had wrapped around the man's mouth and kept it tightly closed.

"Are you dreaming, Shane?" a voice asked him. Cold, a terribly cold breath stung Shane's ear and he couldn't bring himself to turn and see who spoke to him.

He shivered uncontrollably and gagged at the smell of rot which filled the room.

"Where do you think he will end up?" the stranger asked. "Will you guess?"

Shane managed to shake his head.

A cruel laugh, filled with malice rang out, and Shane nearly wet himself with fear.

"He will go up and up and up," the voice said. "Far and away. Alive and not dead. Dead and not alive. You'll understand one day, Shane. Yes. I promise one day you will understand."

Shane closed his eyes and fought the urge to run.

Warmth returned to the room, and the smell of rot faded. Shane could no longer hear footsteps, or the man being dragged down the floor.

Muffled laughter drifted down from the unused servants' quarters, and Shane desperately wished for his parents to return home.

Chapter 32: Alone

Marie Lafontaine had left and promised to return after her shift the following day.

Shane sat on his bed, a glass of whiskey in one hand and his father's belt in the other. He took a small sip and examined the silver buckle.

It was his father's. Shane was certain of it.

The leather was the same as well.

And neither of them was old.

Shane drank a little more.

How is this even possible? He wondered. *My father can't be alive. No matter what anyone says. Maybe trapped, spiritually. But they can't be alive.*

He put the belt down on the bed, finished his whiskey and poured himself another.

The phone in the library rang sharply.

Shane nearly spilled his liquor.

The phone rang again.

He looked out his doorway at the hall.

For a third time, the harsh sound of the telephone cut through the air.

Shane emptied his glass, put it on the table and got up from his bed. Silently, he walked out of his room and to the library.

The black phone on the desktop rang again, which was incredibly interesting.

The phone was an interior line only. No connection to the outside world, only to a phone in the kitchen, and one in the servants' quarters.

And there was no power to the phone. There hadn't been any since Shane had moved into the house as a boy.

Shane walked to the desk, sat down, and picked up the receiver.

"Hello," he said.

"Hello?" a woman asked frantically. "Oh my God, can you hear me?!"

Shane's hands shook. "Yes. Yes, I can hear you."

"Oh thank God," she said, weeping. "Please, I don't know where you are, but I need you to call the police. My husband

and I are trapped in our house. We've been down here for days, and we can't get out."

"Mom?" Shane whispered.

The woman choked back a cry and said, "What? What did you say?"

"Mom," Shane said a little louder. "It's me, Shane."

There was silence on the other end, but Shane could hear his mother breathe.

"Is... is this some kind of trick?" she asked, her tone unsure. "You can't be my son."

"You're Fiona Ryan," Shane said softly. "My father is Hank Ryan. His real name is Henry. He hates it. You only call him Henry when you're mad at him, like when he didn't believe us about the house."

His mother let out a moan. "You can't be Shane. You're too old. You can't be. I can hear how old you are."

"I am old," Shane said. "I'm over forty now, mom."

"No!" She screamed. He jerked his head away from the phone. She spoke again, and he listened once more. "No. No, my Shane is in boot camp. He's graduating in a week. We're going down to South Carolina to see him."

"Mom," he said, his voice growing hoarse, "you've been gone for years. So many years."

The line went dead. Shane sat in the chair and held the silent phone for a moment before he hung it up.

Yet as soon as his hand left the cold handle the phone rang again.

He looked at it cautiously, but by the third ring he picked it up.

"Hello," he said, trying to keep the hope out of his voice.

The harsh laughter which greeted him told him he had failed.

"Shane," a girl said, her voice sounding as if she were speaking from beneath water. "Shane, your parents miss you. Do you miss them?"

Shane hung up the phone and left the library. He closed the door, but even through the thick wood he could hear the telephone ring.

Chapter 33: A Visitor

Someone knocked at the door, and Shane forced his eyes to open.

He was drunk.

Good and drunk. He wasn't sure if it was early afternoon or early morning. Or maybe neither if the clock in the parlor was broken.

He chuckled at the idea of it and managed to get to his feet. He staggered out of the room and into the main hall. Someone knocked again, and the knock was followed by the doorbell.

Shane winced at both sounds, but he still found the image of a broken clock funny. He laughed as he opened the door and then he choked on the laughter.

Christopher Mercurio stood on his doorstep.

He wore the school uniform of Nashua Catholic Junior High School. He even had the trendy, bowl haircut the cooler kids had worn. Christopher Mercurio, the boy who had bullied him in school, even after having hidden in his house, was soaked through as he looked at Shane.

Thoroughly wet, just as he had been when the police had pulled his body out of the pond when Shane was fifteen.

Christopher looked terrified. Confused.

"Am I dead?" he asked Shane.

Shane quickly sobered up.

"Yes, Christopher," Shane said. "You're dead. You have been for a long time."

"She told me I was," Christopher said, and he began to cry. "She told me I can't go home to my parents as they won't want me because I'm dead."

Shane couldn't think of anything to say, so he didn't.

"She killed me, Shane," he said.

"I know."

"You told me not to go near the water," Christopher said, moaning. "You told me not to."

"I know," Shane said sadly.

"I didn't listen to you," the dead boy said, starting to weep. "I wish I'd listened."

"I'm sorry," Shane whispered.

Christopher nodded, wiped his tears away with a wet hand and then he sniffled loudly. "Shane."

"Yes?"

"She's angry," Christopher whispered. "She didn't like it when you hung up on her."

"Did she make you come and tell me?" He asked.

The dead boy nodded.

"Will she let you go now?" Shane asked.

"No," Christopher whimpered. "She never lets any of us go. She says she won't ever let your parents go."

"Are my parents alive, Christopher?" He asked.

"I don't know," the dead boy answered. "I can't tell. I wasn't sure I was dead until I saw you. You're old, Shane. You're bald, too."

Shane nodded.

"I didn't know I was dead. Not for certain. None of us do," Christopher said.

"Are there a lot of you down there, with her?" He asked.

"Yes," the dead boy said. "I'm not sure how many, but there are a lot of us."

"Oh," Shane said.

"She's angry, Shane," Christopher said. "She's so angry. You need to leave, Shane. She's going to hurt you."

"I can't leave. I need my parents," Shane answered.

"She won't let them go," the dead boy sighed. "None of us can go."

Christopher turned and walked away from the door. Shane watched as the dead bully turned to the right and continued on around the house. Back to the pond.

Shane closed the door and returned to his whiskey.

He needed to get drunk again.

Chapter 34: Shane and the Furnace, February 29th, 1988

Shane liked to be in the basement. The basement was safe. Nothing, as far as he could tell, was in the basement.

Yes, it was dark. Yes, there were lots of spiders.

But there weren't any ghosts, and Shane appreciated it tremendously.

The furnace was his favorite part of the basement. The old, oil-run machine was gigantic, a monstrosity which would have looked at home on an old battleship. Shane could picture it running the propeller of some ancient warship.

It was warm by the furnace too. Waves of heat rolled off the hot cast iron casing, and he could catch sight of the flickering red and orange flames as the oil burned.

Shane lay on his back on top of an old woolen army blanket. His book, something by a Chinese general named Sun Tzu, was beside him. He had a bookmark at a page where the general had declared, 'All warfare is deception.' And Shane had a feeling the man knew what he was writing about.

Shane yawned and looked up at rafters and noticed a small box tucked above one of the cross beams. He got to his feet and squinted to try to get a better look at it. He could just make out a single word.

Map.

"Shane!" his mother yelled down the stairs. "Time for lunch!"

"Okay, Mom!" he called back up. He turned towards the stairs.

"And don't leave your book and blanket down there this time," she said.

Shane groaned inwardly, turned around and picked up both of his things. He grumbled to himself and went upstairs.

I'll have to look in the box later, he promised himself, and he turned off the light as he left.

Chapter 35: Remembering

Shane fell out of the chair and landed on the parlor floor with a thud.

Pain blossomed in his head, but he got to his feet.

"The box," he said to the silent room. "The *box!*"

He hurried out of the room, legs unsteady as he approached the main stairs. He cut around to the left, found the hidden pocket door and slid it back. He flipped on the lights and walked quickly down the stairs into the basement.

The air was warm and dry, the furnace rumbled, and there were fewer spider webs than Shane remembered.

He went to stand in front of the furnace where he used to lay down his blanket and looked up.

There was the box. The one with the word *map* written on it.

The one he had never come back to look at.

Shane reached up and grabbed the box. It was an old cigar box. *Hoeffler's Havana's.* A buxom Cuban woman smiled at him and held out a glowing cigar. Shane ignored the advertisement's offer and hoped there was more than old cigars in the box.

There was.

Folded into a neat square was a thick piece of paper.

Shane took it out, set the box on the floor at his feet and unfolded the map. Six-floor plans were sketched out in minute detail. The top left plan had the legend, *Main Floor*, written beneath it. The second, *Second Floor*. Then *Servants' Quarters,* followed by *The Music Room, Where We Fear to Tread,* and *Her Room.* In the far right corner was a small square labeled, *The Root Cellar.* A question mark was beside it.

Shane carried the map upstairs and into the kitchen. He laid it on the table, started a fresh pot of coffee and returned to the map. He held onto both edges of the table and looked down at the paper. He needed to see how to get to the fifth floor, and from there to the sixth.

Nowhere in the Servants' quarters did he see a door marked stairs.

He looked at the second floor and stopped.

The painting, he thought. Set in the wall was a door he had only seen once. The door behind the painting. The stairs which led to the fifth floor.

A quick examination of the fifth floor showed another set of stairs which led up to her rooms.

"Where did you find it?" Carl asked, and Shane nearly jumped.

He turned and saw his dead friend in the chair across from him.

"The basement," Shane answered. He walked over to the coffee, resisted the natural urge to offer the man coffee, and poured himself a cup. He sat down at the table, had a drink and looked at Carl. *"Did you know of it?"*

"Of it? Yes. Where it was? No. I did not know where you might be able to find it if it even existed anymore."

"Who made it?" Shane asked.

"A boy named Herman. A very smart boy. When he realized what was happening in the house, he mapped what he could and then he fled. Not before his mother killed his father, though."

"When was this?"

"Nineteen fifty-two," Carl answered. *"His father was the chauffeur. His mother was a scullery maid. All of them lived together on the third floor."*

"How did he find about all of these?" Shane asked.

"He traveled them," Carl said.

"Is he still alive?" He asked excitedly.

The dead German shrugged. *"I do not know, my young friend."*

"What was his last name?" Shane asked.

"Mishal," Carl answered. *"Herman Mishal."*

Chapter 36: With the Benefit of Years

Herman Mishal took off his glasses, pinched his nose and sighed to no one in particular.

His wife, Bernadette, looked up from her book.

"Are you alright?" she asked in Hebrew.

"Yes," he said with a smile. *"I'm tired. And I do not feel especially well."*

The cordless phone rang, and both he and Bernadette looked at it, surprised.

It was well after ten and the phone never rang after eight. Not unless it was an emergency with one of their children.

Herman put his glasses back on and looked at the caller id.

It read 'unavailable.'

He frowned and answered the phone. "Hello?"

"Hello," a man said. "I hate to bother you this late, but I'm looking for a man named Herman Mishal. Do I have the right house?"

"You do," Herman said. "But, it is terribly late. Perhaps you can call back tomorrow?"

"Sir," the stranger said, a note of anxiety in his voice. "Could you spare me just a minute? Please? It's about my parents?"

"Who is it?" Bernadette asked.

Herman shrugged his shoulders. "Well, you have an advantage. You know my name, but I don't know yours."

"I'm sorry. My name is Shane Ryan."

Nothing about the name was familiar to Herman. "I don't think we know each other, Mr. Ryan."

"We don't," Mr. Ryan said. "But you can help me. I know you can."

"How do you know that?" Herman asked. The mantle of therapist dropped over him.

"I found your map," the man said.

Herman shook his head, confused. "Map? What map are you talking about?"

"The map of the Anderson House."

A chill ripped through Herman and his mouth went dry.

"Herman?" Bernadette said fearfully. "Are you alright?"

He held up a shaky hand to her and nodded slightly. He cleared his throat and asked, "How did you come upon that map, Mr. Ryan?"

"I first saw it when I was a boy," he said. "But I remembered it a little while ago, and I found it in the basement, by the furnace."

Herman's heart pounded against his chest. He whispered, "Where are you, Mr. Ryan?"

"I'm in my house," the man said. "One twenty-five Berkley Street. I need to know how you made it through to her."

"Mr. Ryan," Herman said. "Do you know Nashua at all?"

"Yes," he replied.

"My wife and I live at twenty-six Sherman Street. Would you like to bring the map to me so we can discuss it?"

"Yes," he said, sighing. "Yes. When?"

"Right now," Herman said.

"Yes. I'll be there soon," Mr. Ryan said. "Thank you."

The man disconnected the call, and Herman hung up the phone.

"Herman," Bernadette said sharply. "Why did you invite a stranger here, especially now?"

Herman looked at his wife and smiled weakly. "He lives in the Anderson House."

Her eyes widened, and she closed her mouth tightly. She marked her place in her book, set it aside and stood up. "I'll go put on some coffee."

"Thank you," Herman said. He looked down at his hands, at the fingers which still ached from when they had been broken by *her*.

By the girl in the pond.

Chapter 37: Looking for a Ride

Gerald didn't sleep well.

Age, memories, being a widower.

It all contributed to his insomnia.

Turk, of course, had no such concerns or worries. The dog put his head down on his crossed paws, and fell asleep.

Gerald looked over at the German Shepherd and smiled. Turk lay on his side in front of the hearth, and occasionally his back leg kicked out. Gerald closed his book, set it on the coffee table and picked up his bottle of beer. It was warm, and barely palatable, but he drank it anyway.

The doorbell rang, and Turk was up and on his feet in a heartbeat. The dog's hackles were raised, and his lips pulled back as he growled. His old, yellow teeth still looked fearsome in the room's soft light.

Gerald put the bottle down, opened the drawer to the side-table and pulled the Colt .45 out. He chambered a round and stood up. The doorbell rang again as he left the room and went to the front door.

He stayed out of the sidelights, kept the weapon down by his leg and called out, "Who is it?"

"Gerald, it's me, Shane."

The younger man's voice was urgent and desperate.

Gerald slipped the safety on and stepped up to the door. Within a moment, Shane stepped in, and Turk greeted the man with a lopsided smile while his tail thumped steadily on the floor.

"What's going on?" Gerald asked, gesturing towards the study with the pistol.

"I need a favor," Shane said, dropping into a chair.

The man looked pale, as though he hadn't slept in days and something had run him ragged.

"What?" He asked, returning the Colt to the side-table before sitting down again.

"Could you give me a ride?" Shane asked desperately. "I can give you money for gas, I just, I just can't wait for a taxi."

"Shane," Gerald said, trying to keep his voice relaxed. "Is everything okay?"

The younger man shook his head. "I found a map, in the house. It might lead to my parents. Or, at least, where their bodies are."

Gerald rubbed the back of his head. "A map. What kind of map?"

Shane reached into the front pocket of his sweatshirt and withdrew a folded piece of paper. His hands shook has he handed it over.

Gerald looked at it and tried to make sense of the drawing.

"Shane," he said, "your house doesn't have six floors."

Shane nodded. "I know. It's not supposed to, but it has a lot of things it shouldn't. And this map was made by someone named Herman."

"Herman Mishal," Gerald whispered. He looked down at the paper in his hands. "I remember him. He was a younger, Jewish fellow. But he was a hell of a baseball player. What happened to his parents was terrible."

"I'm sorry," he said, shaking his head and forcing himself to return to the issue. "Shane, where do you need a ride to?"

"To Herman Mishal's house," Shane answered.

Gerald blinked several times and then he asked, "Are you serious?"

He nodded. "I spoke with him maybe ten or fifteen minutes ago. I told him what I had found. He said to come right over. He lives here in Nashua. Twenty-six Sherman Street."

"You need a ride to Herman Mishal's house?" Gerald asked.

"Yes," Shane said. "Please, Gerald."

"Of course," Gerald said, standing up. "Let's go see Herman."

Chapter 38: Meeting the Mishals

Shane was out of Gerald's old Buick before the car was even put into 'park.'

Herman Mishal's house was a small New England cape with a breezeway connecting the main structure to the two car garage. The light of the half-moon glowed in the pale blue siding, and smoke curled up from the chimney.

From either side of the front door, the exterior lamps cast their yellowish light onto the snow, and Shane approached the door excitedly.

He paused though, as he heard Gerald turn off the car's engine. He waited until the older man caught up with him before the two of them walked up the steps.

Nervously, Shane knocked on the door.

A moment later it opened, and a woman who looked to be slightly younger than Gerald smiled at them.

"Come in, please," she said, stepping aside.

Both Shane and Gerald murmured their thanks and entered the house. Warm air wrapped around them, as did the smell of coffee. Every wall, Shane noticed, was lined with bookcases, and each bookcase was neatly organized.

The woman smiled at Shane and said, "We like to read."

Gerald chuckled and nodded his head. "Yes, ma'am, it certainly seems like you do."

"I'm Bernadette Mishal," she said, offering her hand.

Shane and Gerald each shook it in turn while introducing themselves. Bernadette looked at Shane and said, "You live in the house?"

"Yes," he answered.

She nodded, and then she smiled. "Come with me, please. Herman is waiting for you."

They followed her down a narrow hallway, and into a small room. Like the hall, the room was lined with bookcases. Some of the shelves, however, were occupied with family photographs and antiques. The shades were drawn over the room's two windows, and a pair of well-worn reading chairs flanked a small table.

A small, delicate man sat wrapped in a blanket. He marked his page and set his book down on a side-table before he smiled at them.

"Forgive me, please," he said. "I cannot easily get up and out of the chair. I am Herman Mishal."

"Shane Ryan," Shane said, stepping forward and offering his hand.

Herman slipped a hand free of his blanket and carefully shook it.

The older man's fingers, Shane saw, had been severely broken at some point and not set properly.

"Don't be afraid of hurting them," Herman chuckled. He shook out Gerald's hand and nodded to Bernadette. The woman left the room and returned a moment later with a pair of folding chairs.

Shane went to help her, and she looked over her glasses at him sternly.

"Thank you," she said, smiling impishly, "but I am quite adept at doing things my husband should."

"... *wicked girl*," Herman said, and Shane managed to catch only the last of what the man said. It was a language he hadn't heard much of before.

"*... only for you, Herman*," Bernadette said. "*Should I bring the coffee now or would you rather wait?*"

"*If you don't mind*," Shane said, trying out the language, getting used to the harsh sounds and the tricks of the tongue, "*I would prefer a cup of coffee now.*"

All three of them looked at him in surprise.

"You speak Hebrew?" Herman asked.

"I do now," Shane said.

"*What do you mean you do now?*" Herman asked, pronouncing his words carefully. "*Did you not speak it before?*"

"*No*," Shane said, shaking his head. "*But if I hear something, especially the older I get, the easier languages become.*"

"Impressive," Herman said softly. He smiled. "My apologies, though. My wife and I tend to speak Hebrew primarily in the house, so it is only natural for us to lapse into it. I hope I didn't offend either of you."

"No offense taken," Gerald said, smiling.

Bernadette finished setting up the pair of chairs and he and Gerald each sat down. She slipped out of the room to fetch the coffee.

"So," Herman said, sadness in his voice. "You found my map."

Shane nodded.

"And you want to know if it's real," Herman continued, "and whether or not you can use it to retrieve your parents."

"Yes," Shane whispered.

"I can assure you it is real," Herman said. "But as to whether or not you can use it to find your parents, well, I don't know. First, though, may I see the map?"

Shane took the map out, fought down the urge to keep it to himself, and reluctantly handed it over.

Herman freed his other hand from the blanket, and Shane saw those fingers were just as twisted as the others.

The man opened the map, which shook ever so slightly in his grasp, and he sighed sadly. He looked upon the paper for a long time, and then he nodded, folded the map, and returned it to Shane.

Shane tucked it away.

"Did you really make it?" Gerald asked.

"Yes," Herman said, smiling gently. Bernadette entered the room with a small serving tray and four cups of coffee, a sugar bowl and a small pitcher of cream. She handed a cup to each man, added cream and sugar to Herman's and then she turned to Shane and Gerald.

"Would either of you care for cream or sugar?" she asked.

"No thank you," Shane said, taking a cautious sip. The coffee was hot and rich. He sighed happily.

"No thank you, ma'am," Gerald said.

She nodded, put her own cup down on a small table and added sugar. She left the room with the tray and returned a moment later. After she had taken her seat, Herman smiled at her and started to speak.

"I made the map when I was thirteen years old," he said, his voice strong. "I lived in the servants' quarters at one twenty-five Berkley Street. My father, Barney, was the Andersons' butler. My mother, Anna, was a maid. My father was not Jewish, but my mother was. She was insistent about my being raised in the faith, and my father adored her. He was not terribly fond of the Lutheran church."

Herman smiled. "We moved into the estate when I was ten, and we lived there together for five years. The Andersons were kind enough to ensure I received a proper education. Mr. Anderson, who was truly a frightening man, discovered my love of books, and he was kind enough to grant me unrestricted access to his library.

"A little too bellicose for my taste," Herman said with a sigh, "but the books were of the best sort. The way they were bound and written. The array of languages. Anyway, I'm rambling."

"When I was thirteen," he paused and took a sip of his coffee and smiled his thanks to his wife, "I discovered secret ways within the house. They branched off from the servants' passages running through the walls. There were rooms I knew you couldn't find from the halls. Whole floors magically appearing.

"I tried to tell my parents, but neither of them was terribly imaginative, and they merely patted me on the head and told me to concentrate on my studies and not on fairy tales. As time passed, though, I decided to map out my travels. I felt like Shackleton, exploring the great unknown. Sherlock, investigating mysteries. Watson, keeping a journal of all I experienced."

Herman sighed and looked down at his twisted hands. "There was so much more, though. A danger lurking in the walls. One I never expected or even dreamed of. You found it, though, didn't you?"

Shane nodded. "You kept a journal?"

"I did," Herman said. "I have it put away in a safety deposit box. When I pass away, it can be read."

"I remember you," Gerald said, nodding to Herman. "I remember you were one hell of a baseball player."

Herman grinned a youthful, boyish grin. "I loved baseball. I still do. My poor Bernadette has suffered through years of it. When the Red Sox finally won the World Series, she told me I shouldn't ever watch the sport again."

"He didn't listen," Bernadette said. "He was yelling again at the television on opening day the following season."

Herman chuckled, adjusted his glasses and said, "Yes. I yell at the television."

"He doesn't understand they can't hear him," she said.

"It's why I don't watch football anymore," Gerald said. "They don't listen to me."

Herman nodded. "Very true. And yes, I was a fair baseball player. You ask, I suppose, because of my hands?"

"Yes," Gerald said.

The gleam in Herman's eyes died and all the humor was gone from his voice. "She did this."

"Which she?" Shane asked, leaning forward.

"The girl in the pond. Vivienne," he answered.

"How?" Shane asked in a whisper. "How did she do it?"

Herman closed his eyes, took a deep breath and then he said, "She possessed my mother."

Shane's hands shook so badly he had to put his coffee cup on the floor. He clasped his hands together and looked down at his feet.

"It happened to you?" Herman asked.

Shane nodded. "Not with my mother. One of the neighbors who came over to find her lost cat.

Chapter 39: Shane, August 15th, 1988

Shane had known Mrs. Kensington since he had moved into the old Anderson house. She had been the first neighbor to welcome them, and the first to become friends with his mother. Occasionally, he would even go to her house after school if his mom felt particularly uncomfortable about the house.

Mrs. Kensington, in turn, rarely visited their home.

She was never at ease, or so Shane had heard her say. Something bothered her. She couldn't, she had told his mother, quite put her finger on it.

Shane could, of course, and his mother could as well.

On Monday morning, Shane sat at the small kitchen table. In the hall, the grandfather clock struck seven, and he yawned.

Too early, he thought. But the three of them were supposed to be going to Wells, Maine to enjoy the beach.

Shane didn't like the beach, though. Not since he had read *Jaws* and seen the movie. He had even told his mom, but she had said he couldn't stay home alone for the week. His parents had rented a house right on Moody Beach, and Shane was going to be there. He could read all day from the safety of the rented home's porch and not have to worry about sharks.

With a sigh, Shane pushed the last of his egg onto his toast, ate both in one large bite that his mother would have reprimanded him for, and stood up. He chewed as he walked, which certainly would have earned him a second scolding, if not an outright punishment, and carried his plate to the sink. He rinsed off the yolk, put the dish amongst the others, and walked to the back door.

He opened it and looked at the backyard.

As always, it was quiet outside, but he couldn't see the girl in the pond. Some mornings, she lurked near the surface; a hideous white form beneath the water. While others, she disappeared completely.

Nothing, though, and Shane smiled.

"Captain!" A voice called out, nearly startling Shane.

He looked to the right, and he saw Mrs. Kensington. The woman wore a pair of khaki gardening shorts, a button down blue shirt, and a wide-brimmed sun hat over her pinned up gray hair. She was short and stout and at times she looked almost like a bulldog the way her jowls would hang down. But her smile was always genuine, and she made the best chocolate chip cookies Shane had ever eaten. He didn't mind the pair of Birkenstock sandals she wore, which she had probably purchased just after the end of the nineteen sixties. For some reason, they drove his father crazy though.

As did the name of her orange cat.

Captain.

"Captain!" She called again.

Shane watched as she approached the pond, but since he couldn't see the girl in the water, he didn't worry too much about it.

He didn't think the cat was in the yard, either. Most animals stayed away from one twenty-five Berkley Street. And those few who wandered in usually ran away after a minute or two on the property.

Mrs. Kensington's head turned towards the pond and Shane heard her say, "Captain?"

He could hear the rustle of the tall grass around the water's edge, and evidently Mrs. Kensington heard it as well. She took a step closer.

"Captain," she said. "What are you doing by the water?"

A white, swollen hand, streaked with mud and filth, suddenly shot out of the grass, latched onto Mrs. Kensington's thick ankle and pulled.

Shane threw open the screen door as Mrs. Kensington was jerked into the water. The splash was loud and frightening. He heard her cough and splutter. She slapped at the water, and a scream was ripped from her.

He hurried down the back steps and sprinted to the pond. Mrs. Kensington clung to the bank and dug her fingers into the grass. She pulled up great clumps of it as she dragged herself forward. She was wet and filthy, and when Shane finally reached her, he quickly helped her to her feet. He hauled her back to the house and got her into the kitchen.

The screen door slammed behind them as he led her to the table. Shane sat her down in the seat he had so recently vacated and ran to the sink. He poured a glass of cold water and carried it to her before grabbing a hand towel off a hanger by the fridge.

Mrs. Kensington was covered in mud, her clothes stained with it. She looked dully at the glass in front of her. Shane wrinkled his nose as he got closer. The mud stank of rot and filth.

"Here, Mrs. Kensington," he said, holding the towel out to her.

She blinked several times before she turned and looked at him. Her face was slack, her eyes vacant. Her hat, he noticed, was gone and strands and clumps of her gray hair had escaped the bun she had tied it in.

"Mrs. Kensington?" Shane asked.

She smiled.

A cold, hard smile.

Her eyes focused and locked onto him.

"Hello Shane," she said, and yet it wasn't Mrs. Kensington who spoke.

It was Vivienne.

"This body is old. It is fat," the dead girl said as she pushed away from the table and stood on uncertain legs. "However, it will suffice."

She licked her lips.

"Oh," Vivienne whispered. "She likes you, Shane. She does. Dirty little thoughts about a dirty little boy."

Vivienne laughed, and it was a harsh, painful sound.

Shane winced and took a cautious step towards the hallway.

"Where will you go?" She asked. "To a bedroom? It's what she wants. Shall we give it to her, Shane?"

The door between the hall and the kitchen slammed closed.

Vivienne blocked his path to the back door.

"No," she said softly. "I don't think we'll give her anything except your death, Shane. A brilliant memory of her murdering you. A gift to your mother as well. Do you think dear mother will make it from the bathroom to the kitchen without falling? I'm certain she'll race naked as the day she was born when she hears Mrs. Kensington scream.

"And Mrs. Kensington will scream, Shane," Vivienne hissed. "When she sees your body, and realizes it was she who killed you."

Vivienne lunged at him.

Shane didn't try to slip to the right or to the left.

Instead, he charged at her.

Vivienne's eyes widened in surprise, and a small grunt escaped her lips as he struck her solidly in the chest.

Shane was small, but he had faced more bullies than he cared to remember.

And none of his tormentors ever expected him to charge at them.

Vivienne was dead, but she was still nothing more than a bully.

She staggered back, and Shane raced for the back door.

Which slammed shut.

Vivienne screamed with rage, and he spun around to face her.

"You'll pay," she spat.

"Shut up," Shane said, grinning.

Her eyes widened and her face reddened. "What?"

"Shut up," Shane repeated. "Shut up. You're nothing. A dead brat. Nothing else. And you smell like dead fish."

Vivienne shrieked and blood exploded out of Mrs. Kensington's nose. The older woman's body lurched towards him, and Shane waited until the last moment to move. He ducked easily under the flabby arms and let out a frightened laugh as Vivienne slipped and slammed into the wall.

The door to the kitchen burst open, and Shane's mother ran in.

She had on her bathrobe, but water dripped from her body and from her hair. She looked at Mrs. Kensington in surprise and said, "Beatrice?!"

The woman came to a stop, shuddered, blinked, and stumbled back into the wall.

The entire house shook, and Shane heard the front door slam open, and his father yell.

The world went black in front of Shane, and he felt himself fall.

Chapter 40: What to do about the Map?

Shane cracked his knuckles nervously. He caught sight of Herman's fingers and stopped.

Herman chuckled. "Don't worry about my feelings, Shane. Your nervous habit won't bother me."

Shane smiled his thanks.

Herman pulled his blanket around him and settled back into his chair. "When I was fifteen years old, my mother made the mistake of going too close to the pond. Well, at least that is what I assumed happened. No one saw her prior to the murder, you see."

"I was home, after school, and I was practicing with my violin. My mother came into the apartment, and she was... well, she was different." He sighed and closed his eyes. "She smelled. That curious, foul smell peculiar to the pond behind the house. I should have known then something was wrong. But, I was fifteen. I was focused solely upon my violin. And when I wasn't seeing Schubert's music, I was picturing the upcoming game against Dracut High School.

"I first realized something was amiss when my mother ripped the violin out of my hands. She had a grin, a smile full of teeth which didn't look quite right on my mother's face. Before I could ask her what was wrong, she struck me on the head."

"Herman," Bernadette said.

He opened his eyes and smiled at his wife. "I am alright, my love. Thank you."

"Now," he continued, "she struck me on the head. A terrific blow which knocked me off the stool and onto the floor. Before I could get to my hands and knees, she struck me several more times. She shattered the instrument, I am afraid, and I must have been knocked unconscious. I later awoke to excruciating pain. My mother was stomping upon my fingers with her heels.

"It was then my father entered the apartment. I must have been screaming. He was followed by one of the gardeners. It was he who pulled me away from my mother while my father attempted to gain control over her. Or, rather, the evil inside of her."

Herman paused and smiled sadly at them. "Unfortunately, the girl in the pond had quite the grip upon my mother. When he grabbed her, my mother tore his throat out with her teeth.

"The gardener was a smart man and instantly realized something was wrong. He slammed the door shut and locked it. Since my mother was Jewish, they called for a Rabbi. Unfortunately, the closest Rabbi was at Temple Adath Yeshurun in Manchester. I was brought to St. Joseph's Hospital, for my hands to be looked at. By the time the Rabbi reached the Andersons' house, my mother had died.

"She choked to death on my father's heart."

"Good God," Gerald said, crossing himself.

"I did not appreciate God for quite some time," Herman said. He looked at Shane. "Did she speak to you, when she tried to kill you?"

Shane nodded. "She told me some of the things Mrs. Kensington was thinking."

"Yes," Herman said. "She did the same with my mother. Who knows what was truth and what was fiction. I can only assume she used a fine mixture of both. The most hurtful lies are those with a bit of honesty in them."

Silence fell over all of them for a few minutes.

"Well," Herman said. "Since we have now established our credentials regarding one twenty-five Berkley Street, how may I help you, Mr. Ryan?"

"I need you to explain your map to me," Shane said. "I need to get to her."

"Why?" Herman asked.

"Because," Shane said with a sigh. "She still has my parents."

And he explained to Herman and Bernadette and Gerald what had happened to his mother and father.

Chapter 41: Marie Finds She Must Believe

It had taken Marie ten years to beat alcohol. She had moments, of course, where she wanted a drink. Hell, moments when she *needed* a drink.

But every alcoholic wrestled with the need.

Marie had never, however, been so close to breaking her sobriety.

Something was wrong with the Anderson House. Something inside of it was bad. She had enough problems when she went through withdrawal to understand hallucinations and delirium.

What she had experienced in the Anderson House was real. Terrifyingly real.

She got up out of her chair, walked over to her bonsai trees and inspected them. She had already taken care of her miniature grove in the morning. When she stood in front of the trees, though, she felt peaceful.

It helped take her mind off the rum and coke.

She glanced at the clock on the wall.

One, she read. Her stomach growled, as she gave it a pat. It was time to eat, and she was hungry.

Nevertheless, her experiences with Shane Ryan dominated her thoughts.

None of it could be real, and yet it was. She couldn't deny it.

I want to, she thought, turning away from the trees. *Oh, Christ do I want to.*

Because if she couldn't deny it, she had to accept it. And if she accepted it, it meant she had experienced an event the likes of which she had scoffed at for years.

How many calls did I get when I first joined the Nashua Police Department where nothing had been found? People adamant they'd heard something, seen something? She thought.

The jokes with the other cops about people who drank too much, as they sat in their favorite bar and consumed massive amounts of alcohol to deal with the other, more horrific events. Painful crimes which had been all too real.

And now this, she thought.

Marie walked back to her chair and sat down. She looked at the television and realized she didn't want to watch anything. She glanced over at her computer. Her screensaver, a photo of her trees, cast a soft light over her desk.

She had played solitaire for hours, and contemplated playing a few more. She had to be at court for the Jubert case at nine. Otherwise she was free.

Free to sit and obsess over the Anderson House.

After court, she told herself. *After court, I'll go back and see Shane. We'll figure out what's going on. I'll talk to Uncle Gerry, too. He's been on Berkley Street for as long as I can remember.*

I bet he knows something.

Marie stood and went to the kitchen. She needed something to eat before she played another hour's worth of solitaire.

Chapter 42: Shane, April 9th, 1989

Shane no longer let his parents put his bureau in front of the door that Eloise and Thaddeus used. For some reason, the noisy piece of furniture being pushed across the floor was worse than when either of the ghosts whispered in his ear.

He stayed out of the pantry, if he could help it, and away from the root cellar's trap door at all costs. Occasionally he could hear the dark ones whisper.

And it was never pleasant.

Ever.

The library was safe. So was the parlor. He didn't trust the kitchen, not since Mrs. Kensington had been possessed by Vivienne.

He felt badly for Mrs. Kensington, too. She couldn't look at him and, not surprisingly, his mother didn't have the woman watch him anymore.

I don't need watching, Shane thought. He tied his sneakers and stood up. A glance out the window showed dark clouds. The sun was hidden, and by the looks of the clouds, there might be a thunderstorm.

Downstairs a door slammed.

Shane turned away from the window and looked out into the hallway.

Both of his parents were out, and the ghosts hadn't slammed any doors in a couple of years.

With the exception of Vivienne.

"Carl?" Shane said softly.

Carl didn't answer.

"Eloise?"

Silence.

"Thaddeus?"

He knew better than to call for Roberto. The musician barely heard anything. He played too often and was too far away. Occasionally, Shane would catch a bit of music, but only once in a great while.

Shane walked out of his room to the top of the stairs.

Heavy scrapes dragged through the air, and someone slammed a piece of furniture down.

Shane walked a few steps down.

"My friend?" he whispered in German.

Still Carl didn't answer.

The old man in his parents' bathroom moaned and caused Shane's heart to leap.

His head started to pound, and he walked down to the main hall.

More noise came out of the parlor.

The door, he saw, was closed. The light flickered in a mad rhythm from under it and shadows shifted crazily across the wood floor.

Shane nervously licked his lips and reached for the door.

Something cold and hard grasped his wrist and stopped him.

Surprised, he looked to the right, and a moment later a man appeared. An old man stood tall and gaunt. He wore a black suit and his white hair hung past his shoulders. His blue eyes shined, and his lips parted to reveal a mouthful of broken, yellowed teeth.

"Away, boy!" the man hissed, and Shane recognized the voice.

The old man.

The old man. The one from his parents' room.

"Away!" the old man said again. "You don't know what's in there. You don't want to know. Get out!"

A deep, hideous voice screamed through the parlor door. The thing said a name Shane didn't catch, but evidently the old man did.

A second later his wrist was free, and the man from the bathroom was gone.

Before Shane could move the door to the parlor was ripped open, and death stood in front of him.

A skeleton, bones yellowed, lurched towards him and Shane stumbled backward. It was barren of clothing, yet wisps of black hair clung to its skull. The dead man howled while reaching for Shane as he scrambled out of the way. The skeleton's bones scraped across the floor, and Shane got to his feet and ran.

He sprinted down the hall, tripped over his own feet and slammed into the wall by the kitchen door. A look back showed the skeleton only a few paces away.

Shane lunged for the kitchen, but a bony hand locked onto his shirt collar and jerked him back. A terrible chill swept through him and Shane shivered violently. His stomach churned, and the Fruit Loops he'd eaten for breakfast rushed up his throat and burned his mouth as he vomited over the floor.

The skeleton shrieked with glee and Shane felt himself being lifted off the floor and thrown back down the hall. He struck the wood, and his head spun. He gasped for breath as he was elevated again and darkness finally rushed over him.

**

Pain woke Shane up and made him realize he was alive.

With a groan, he pushed himself up from the floor. He rubbed his eyes with the palms of his hands until stars exploded behind his eyelids. The iron tang of blood filled his mouth, and his nose hurt. Shane got to his feet and walked haphazardly to the sitting room's main bathroom. The grandfather clock struck one, and he dimly realized he'd been knocked out for hours.

Shane turned on the light and leaned over the old porcelain sink. He ran the cold tap, splashed water against his face and rinsed out his mouth. Blood circled the drain and a piece of his tooth clattered against the metal.

Shane probed his teeth with his tongue but couldn't feel anything exceptionally painful. Everything was sore, and he felt as though someone had beaten him.

Someone did, Shane thought with a sigh. *They were just dead.*

He rinsed his mouth out once more, cleaned the blood and turned the water off as he straightened up. He looked at his reflection and blinked several times.

I'm different, Shane thought.

It was almost horror flick different.

His face was swollen. Both eyes were black and blue. One whole cheek was swollen and red. The other was scratched.

And all of his hair was gone.

Every single strand on his head.

All of it was gone.

His eyebrows were gone. The eyelashes. The hint of a mustache and the few scrawny hairs which had populated his cheeks. All of them were gone.

Shane looked down at his arms and saw they were smooth and bare as well. He leaned over and pulled up the leg of his pants. Horrified, he watched as his leg hair fell and clung to his sock and his sneaker.

He let his pants' leg fall and sat down on the toilet. The skin of his scalp was warm and smooth under his hand, as though he had never had hair.

For the first time, in a long time, Shane cried.

Chapter 43: A Decision is Made

"Are you sure about this?" Bernadette asked, fixing his tie for him.

"Of course not," Herman said. His stomach twisted nervously. Fortunately, he had not been able to eat anything. If he had, he would have been in the bathroom, on his knees, with a sincere worry as to whether or not he would be sick.

"Then why?" She asked, looking at him.

"I must," he said. *"Not only for him but myself, my love. His parents are dead, of course, but he should know for certain."*

Bernadette nodded, finished his tie, and stepped back. She smiled at him proudly. *"So handsome, my beautiful husband."*

Herman blushed, as he always did. As he always would.

"Are you ready?" she asked.

He nodded.

Bernadette put on her coat, took her purse and the car keys off the shelf by the back door, and led the way out.

A few minutes later, they were in their old Chevy sedan and Bernadette took her time. Berkley Street was only a few minutes away, and Herman knew she had no desire to see him return to the house.

His stomach twisted around and seemed to push against his ribs.

The fear grew with every rotation of the tires. With every foot, every inch they drew closer to the house. To where his mother, possessed, killed his father and eventually herself.

Gluttony, Herman thought.

He remembered the Rabbi and of being forced to go and live with his mother's sister. A kind woman, but not his mother.

No, not his mother.

Tears welled up in Herman's eyes, and he quickly blinked them away.

Bernadette didn't bring him to the Anderson House, but instead she drove to Gerald's house. When she pulled into the older man's driveway, the door to the house opened, and Shane Ryan hurried out.

The man looked tired, battered.

Herman, who had spent a lifetime as a therapist, could only imagine the prolonged horror the man had suffered through.

Bernadette turned the engine off and looked at Herman.

"Is Gerald going in with you?" she asked.

"I don't believe so," Herman said. "Let me ask, though."

He opened the door and got out of the car.

"Good morning," Shane said.

"Good morning," Herman said, smiling in an effort to hide his growing fear. "My wife would like to know if Gerald will be accompanying us?"

"No," Shane answered, shaking his head.

Bernadette got out of the car. She had the keys and her purse. "I will ask if I can stay here with Gerald then."

"Are you certain?" he asked her.

She smiled. *"What do you think?"*

Chapter 44: Going into the House

Shane stood with Herman in Gerald's kitchen.

Gerald, Turk and Bernadette were in the study.

Shane looked at the old man with the crippled fingers and asked again, "Are you sure about this, Herman? I just wanted to know the best way into the house."

"I'm sure, Shane," Herman answered. "And, quite honestly, I am the best path into the other rooms of the house. I knew them all when I was a boy. I may have forgotten one or two, but I doubt it.

"They were terrifying."

Shane nodded in agreement.

The doorbell rang and Turk barked from the study.

A moment later, Gerald exited the room with a frown on his face. He hurried to the front door, peered through the sidelight and let out a surprised, but pleased laugh. Quickly he threw back the deadbolt and let Marie Lafontaine in.

"You weren't supposed to be over until later this afternoon," Gerald said, giving his niece a hug.

She grinned as she nodded. "I know. The Jubert boy pled out. I didn't have to testify."

"Shane and Mr. Mishal were just about to leave, but Mr. Mishal's lovely wife is going to keep me company," Gerald said.

Marie looked at her uncle shrewdly. "You know all about what's going on at Ryan's house, don't you?"

For a moment, it looked as though Gerald would deny it, but then he said, "Yes. I know exactly what has occurred."

"I don't mean to sound rude," Marie said, turning her attention to Herman, "but how do you fit into this?"

Shane looked at the man and saw a mischievous grin steal across his face.

"I'm looking to purchase the home so I might turn it into a school for wayward girls," Herman said evenly.

Marie's eyes widened for a heartbeat before they narrowed.

"No, my dear lady," Herman said, chuckling. "Nothing of the sort. I make jokes when I am afraid, and right now, I am petrified. As to how I fit into the grand scheme of the

Anderson House, well, I lived there as a boy before young Shane did. The house claimed my parents, but in a far different fashion than the way in which it took Shane's. I, at least, have the cold comfort of knowing they died. Shane does not."

The simple truth of Herman's statement struck Shane viciously, and he dropped his chin to his chest.

Herman had summed it up succinctly.

Shane had no idea what happened to his parents. He could only hope they were dead. Part of him, the childish part, wished to find them alive. To find them thus, however, would mean they had spent decades in hell. They would be insane. No one could survive it.

No one.

Shane lifted his chin up. "Thank you, Herman."

"Mr. Mishal," Marie said, offering her hand, "I'm Marie Lafontaine. I'm going to help today."

Herman shook the hand carefully. "I am Herman, Ms. Lafontaine. We are going to need all of the help we can get. Let us walk to the Anderson House, and I will tell you what I know of the fourth floor."

Chapter 45: Herman, August 27th, 1947

"You play beautifully," Herman said to the skeleton in the small music room.

The dead man held a violin loosely and stared at Herman with empty eye sockets.

Doesn't he speak English? Herman wondered. He only spoke English and Hebrew, and he doubted the dead man spoke Hebrew.

Herman wracked his brain and tried to think of a way he could communicate with the musician.

A grin stole across Herman's face. Even though he knew the skeleton couldn't understand him, Herman asked, "May I?"

He pointed to a beautiful, dark stained violin. A bow lay beside it on its shelf, and there was a small jar of resin with it as well.

The skeleton held up its violin in what Herman thought was an inquisitive way.

"Yes," Herman said, nodding. "I can play."

The musician gestured to the wall and nodded.

Happily, Herman picked up the bow. Carefully he added some resin and then he picked up the violin. He tucked it under his chin, adjusted his fingers, and picked out the first part of Schubert's Death and the Maiden, which he was sure he had heard from the room.

After the first few bars, the skeleton joined in, and soon the room was filled with the music of Schubert.

They played together for a long time until sweat gathered at the base of Herman's neck and ran down his spine to pool in the waistband of his underwear. Eventually, the two of them worked their way through the entire piece, and when it was finished the skeleton said, "Bravo!"

The word startled Herman, and he laughed at his own fear.

The musician chuckled as well.

"Can I, can I go through the door?" Herman asked, gesturing with the bow to the door beside the skeleton.

The musician's laughter stopped, and he looked from the door to Herman and cocked his head questioningly.

Herman nodded.

The skeleton pointed to the door with his bow, then brought it back to the violin quickly and dragged it across the strings in a harsh, discordant note. He pointed to the door again.

"Yes," Herman said after a moment. "Something bad is beyond the door."

"Si," the musician said, speaking for the first time. "Il Male. Il Male."

Herman nodded.

From his seat on a high stool, the skeleton pointed at the door, to a whistle which hung beside it.

A dog whistle? Herman thought. He put the violin and the bow back and stepped to the door.

The musician said something he didn't catch, but Herman felt he understood the gist of it.

The whistle was important.

Herman took it down and looped the long string over his neck.

"Il Male," the musician said, and then he teased out a long, high-pitched note from his violin.

"Blow the whistle," Herman said, bringing it up to his lips, "if I see something bad. Il Male."

The musician nodded and repeated the note. When he finished he said, "Il Male."

"Thank you," Herman said. He opened the door and stepped out into a forest.

Chapter 46: Searching for the Entrance

"A forest?" Marie asked as Shane opened the door and led the way into the house.

"Yes," Herman said, stepping inside. "A forest."

"How can a forest be inside of a house?" she asked, confused. She closed the heavy front door and looked at Herman. "How?"

"There are rules, of course," Herman said slowly, as if he picked each word carefully from a giant mental dictionary before he answered. "We know of how things go up, and therefore, they must come down. We know there is a finite amount of space within an area, such as this hall. These are absolutes, correct?"

Marie nodded.

"Excellent," he said. "No, the issue is not a lack of rules within the confines of the house, but *new* rules. Different rules. A room is as large as she wishes it to be. The dead may or may not leave. The dead may or may not be dead. The rules are hers, so we must learn them.

"Now," Herman said, "we must proceed to the second floor."

Shane looked at the older man and instead of going up the stairs, he said, "Herman, are you alright?"

Herman turned to face him, and Shane saw how pale the man's face was. Beads of sweat gathered around the man's temple and a nervous hand adjusted his small, black yarmulke on his head.

"No, Shane," Herman said with a tight smile. "I am not alright. I am terrified at what I'm going to find. This house, not surprisingly, features rather prominently in my nightmares."

"I understand," Shane said.

The older man nodded his head. "I'm sure you do. Now, Ms. Lafontaine, would you be able to lend me your arm? I am always rather cautious with stairs."

"Yes," Marie said, stepping up to his side.

Shane looked at both of them for a minute, the detective and the retired therapist. *They're both here to help me.*

An odd mixture of humility and strength washed over him. Shane smiled a moment later after he recognized it.

He had felt the same thing every time he and his Marines went into combat.

Nothing can beat us, Shane thought, as he led the way up the stairs.

In a short time, they stood before the door to the servants' quarters, and Shane tried the doorknob. It was locked.

"Locked?" Herman asked.

"Yes," Shane said.

"Do you have the key?" the old man asked.

"There isn't one," Shane answered.

"Ms. Lafontaine, could you please go to the window for me?" Herman asked.

"Sure," Marie answered. She walked to the large window at the end of the hall. It, like all of the others in the house, was huge. The sill was nearly a foot deep, and white panels lined the sides.

When she reached the window, Herman said, "Could you please press on the lower left corner of the bottom right panel?"

She leaned forward, pushed on the panel and let out a surprised laugh as the panel swung in. Cautiously, she reached in and pulled out a key and an old baseball.

Shane looked over to Herman and saw the man was smiling.

"Could you bring them both over?" the old man asked.

She nodded and the panel clicked closed as she returned to the servants' door. Herman accepted both the key and the baseball from her.

He looked longingly at the ball and smiled gently. After a moment, he said, "This was my favorite baseball. My absolute favorite. It is signed by Roy Campanella. Do you know him?"

Both Shane and Marie shook their heads.

"A pity," Herman said. He slipped the ball into a pocket of his coat. "I will tell you all about him when we are done here."

The man turned to the door and, with surprising dexterity, considering the state of his fingers, fit the key into the lock.

The door opened effortlessly for him. The faintest strands of music drifted down to them, and a huge smile appeared on Herman's face.

"The musician," he whispered. Then, in a louder voice, Herman said, "Come, we must see the musician for only through his room can we get to the fifth floor. Lead on, young man, lead on."

Shane nodded and went up the stairs.

The hallway on the third floor was dimly lit. A single bulb flickered randomly in the sconce by Roberto's door. The air was cold and stale, and Marie coughed uncomfortably.

"It will be better when he realizes we are here," Herman said.

Shane was about to ask him what he meant, but Roberto answered the unasked question.

All of the lights in the hall burst into life, warmth flooded the air, and the musician's door sprang open. It nearly hit the wall, but it stopped a hair's breadth from the plain plaster.

Music exploded into the room, and Herman laughed happily. He put the key in his pocket and turned to face Shane.

"He is pleased," Herman said, his eyes shining with excitement. "Oh, Shane, Marie, I have not seen the musician in decades. The music we would play together. I learned how to play Vivaldi here, and waltzes. Ah, Marie, the waltzes I could play. And I could dance as well."

The old man went silent, and he looked down at his hands.

"What she took from me," he whispered. "What she took from me."

Shane reached out and put his hand on Herman's shoulder.

The older man looked at him, blinked and said softly, "What she took from us both, eh, Shane?"

Shane nodded. "Do you want to lead the way?"

"Yes," Herman said. "Yes, I do."

Chapter 47: A Meeting of Old Friends

Herman could hardly contain his excitement as he navigated the last few steps to the musician's closed door. Marie was directly behind him, a firm hand on his lower back to make sure he wouldn't fall should his twisted hands refuse to retain their grip on the banisters.

At the last step, he let go of the right railing and knocked gently on the door.

The lock clicked, the doorknob turned, and the portal opened.

Herman looked into the room of the musician and fought back tears.

The walls were still lined with shelves. Each shelf had its violin and its bow. The light was on at the end, and the musician sat upon his stool. The skeleton played beautifully, as always, and the music pulled at Herman's heart.

Shane and Marie entered the room and closed the door behind them.

The musician lowered his violin and looked at them with his hollow eyes. He said something in a language Herman didn't understand.

"He says 'hello, my friend'," Shane said.

Herman wiped a few errant tears away and looked at the younger man. "You understand him?"

Shane nodded. "He's speaking Italian. His name is Roberto Guidoboni."

"Roberto," Herman whispered.

Roberto chuckled and spoke again.

Once more Shane translated.

"He's happy to see us, and hopes Marie doesn't find his appearance too distressing," Shane said.

"I don't," Marie said, although her face was pale.

Roberto spoke again, for a longer time, and when he finished, Shane nodded. He said, "He has often thought of you, Herman. He remembers the music the two of you played together. And he wonders what has brought the three of us to him."

"Could you tell him we need to enter the forest?" Herman asked.

Shane did so.

Roberto looked at the door which led to the forest, and then he looked back to them and spoke.

"He wants to know if we're certain of traveling through the forest," Shane said.

"Yes," Herman answered. "We have no choice, not if we wish to find what happened to your parents."

Shane relayed the answer.

Roberto brought the violin up to his chin and played a few notes. The door to the forest glowed. The lock clicked, and the door swung open.

Marie gasped in surprise and Shane said, "Damn."

"We came through the door," Marie said. "But it was only stone and darkness."

"Because you were in a passage," Herman said. "You can only get to the forest from this room, or from hers. No other way. Shane, will you be kind enough to take the whistle? The one hanging by the door?"

Shane walked to the door and took the whistle down. It was a seaman's whistle, long and thin and attached to a twine cord. Herman shook his head as Shane held it out to him.

"You wear it," he said.

"What is it for?" Shane asked, slipping the long cord over his neck, allowing the whistle to rest against the center of his chest.

"An emergency," Herman answered.

"*Buona fortuna, amico mio,*" Roberto said, and Herman didn't need it to be translated.

He smiled at the musician and stepped through the door, into the forest.

Chapter 48: A Difficult Journey

When the door closed behind them, Shane realized they were locked in the forest.

It was a strange thought, the idea of being locked into something like a forest, but, then again, the Anderson House was far from normal.

He had never quite comprehended just how abnormal it was, though.

The forest, unlike the property around the house, was not silent.

It was filled with the sound of crows, their harsh and dangerous calls in the perpetual twilight.

The air was cold, and the leaves of the trees had changed colors. Yet without the benefit of the sun, the colors were muted and blunt. Shane could faintly smell rot, as though somewhere among all the foliage, some dead animals slowly went the way of all flesh.

"This place is bad," Marie said.

"Very much so," Herman said. He looked at Shane and Marie. "There is nothing delicate about this place, nothing beautiful. In my youth, I came upon the bones of others who had gone before us."

"What do you mean, others?" Marie asked. She looked around. "There are bodies here?"

Herman nodded.

Shane shook his head and let out a sharp laugh.

"What?" Marie asked.

"I wonder if my parents are here, among the trees," he said. "If they died here."

"Is there any way you'll be able to find out?" Marie asked.

"I don't know," Shane said. He felt miserable, as though someone had hung the proverbial millstone around his neck.

"Shane," Herman said.

He looked at the older man. "Yes?"

"I don't believe your parents will be here, in this forest," Herman said. "She would have taken them to her room. It is what she did. I found others there, in her room. Those with whom she had been especially displeased. If she snatched both of your parents, as the dead have told you she did, then they will be in her room. Not here. Not on the forest floor."

Shane looked at Herman for a long time, and then he nodded. "Thank you."

Herman smiled. "Now, let us move quickly. As I said, the rules in the house are different. She has done something, I am not quite sure what. Time, all of it, is different."

"I'll take point," Shane said, "unless you remember the way."

"The way is simple and straightforward," Herman said. "There is but one path and it leads to her room."

Marie looked around, and then she pointed and said, "Is it there?"

Shane followed the line of her finger and saw a slim trail which started between a pair of tall, thick elm trees.

"Yes," Herman said, his voice low. "Yes, Ms. Lafontaine. There it is."

Shane looked at it and felt fear creep into his belly. It was the same fear he'd felt in Afghanistan and Iraq. The same fear which had gnawed on his stomach in Bosnia.

This won't be a stroll through the park, he told himself. *She's waiting. They're all waiting.*

He wished for Carl. Or Eloise and Thaddeus.

Hell, Shane thought. *Even the old man.*

Someone who had dealt with Vivienne more than either he or Herman had.

But such a person wasn't available.

Shane took a deep breath and then his first step.

The second was easier. And within a few feet, he passed through the trees and stepped onto the trail.

The trees closed in around them. Dead brush and wicked briar climbed up between the trunks. They limited what he could see, magnified what he heard.

An angry grumble joined the voices of the crows. Shane could hear Herman and Marie behind him as he scanned the trail from left to right and back again. Occasionally the growth on either side fell away and revealed things he didn't wish to see.

The bones of a child, clad in the remnants of clothing so old he couldn't tell when the child might have been from.

A dog's skull looked at him from a pile of ash.

A woman's skeleton, her tattered dress gathered around her. Her skull was off to one side of a tall tree, and a rough noose still hung from a low branch.

The remains of cats and other animals. Squirrels dead beneath trees. Even the skeleton of a horse, still in its harness and hooked to a two-wheeled carriage.

"Don't look too much," Herman said gently. "You will be drawn in. It is part of the trap. The desire to see what is beyond the path. To learn who they were."

"What happens if you leave the path?" Marie asked.

"I suspect the path vanishes," Herman answered. "No matter what we see we must remain upon the trail. We risk a prolonged death if we deviate. Or at least that is what I believe will happen."

"Well, let's not find out," Marie said. After a moment, she asked, "Herman, what led you in here to begin with?"

Herman paused and then answered, "The ragman."

Chapter 49: Herman, July 14th, 1947

At the edge of the Andersons' property, where it ran into the conservation land of Greeley Park, Herman had found the perfect spot.

The dead end of Chester Street was marked by a large oak tree. The tree was about a foot from the stone pillar which marked the property line of the Andersons. Rose, the kitchen maid, had given him an old flour sack and Herman had tied it up between the stone and the tree.

When it hung down, it made the perfect target to practice his pitches.

Herman paced off the distance from the sack and used a piece of wood to mark the spot where the pitcher's mound would be. He'd even been able to gather up a dozen beat-up baseballs from behind Holman Stadium. They were piled in an old milk bucket and waited for him.

The old flour sack hung limply from its cords, and Herman gave it a nod.

He wasn't throwing to the sack, he was throwing to Harry "the Horse" Danning, the greatest Jewish catcher ever to play in the big leagues.

Herman took a ball out of the bucket and sighed happily at the feel of the old leather in his hands. The stitching soon found its way underneath his fingers and Herman grinned at the Danning.

He went into his windup, let the ball go at just the right moment, and watched with satisfaction as it slapped into the center of the sack. The burlap snapped up and around the ball and dropped it in the tall grass.

"Well, you've got a hell of a good arm there, kid," a voice said from behind Herman.

He turned around and saw the ragman. The old Greek stood with his arms crossed over his broad chest, and he nodded approvingly. At the intersection of the street the ragman's old chestnut mare stood with her head down as she nosed around the grass. His wagon stood still behind her. Buckets of old rags, ready for use, stood open to the warm summer air. Other rags, which needed to be cleaned, were in closed buckets.

"You want to play for the big leagues, maybe the Boston Braves, yes?" the ragman asked.

"Sure I do," Herman said with a smile.

"Who do you throw to there, hm?" the man said.

"Danning," Herman answered.

"Ah, the Jew," the Greek said, nodding. "Yes. He is a very good catcher. Very good. Even though I am Greek, I would throw to him too."

The man laughed, and the sound echoed off the trees and the back of the Anderson house. Herman grinned.

"Got a lot of rags today?" Herman asked.

"Just enough," the ragman said. "Just enough. Tell me, who is in the kitchen today?"

"Rose."

"Ah," the ragman said. "The pretty one?"

Herman blushed slightly as he shrugged. "Maybe."

"Yes," the Greek chuckled. "The pretty one. I will not tell her, do not fear. We men, must not let them know, or they get too strong, yes?"

"Sure," Herman said, grinning.

"I will go up and leave Niki here, yes?" the Greek asked.

"Sure, she can stay," Herman answered.

"She will cheer you on," the ragman said, nodding his head with mock seriousness. "Yes. She will make certain Danning gives you the right signals. No curves, young pitcher. Only fastballs. I know they cannot hit your fastball."

Herman smiled and waved as the Greek whistled and turned towards the house. The man started to cut through the backyard, as Herman bent down to take another baseball out of the bucket. He tossed it easily from one hand to the next as he pictured Danning and the signal for a fastball.

With his foot against the board, Herman went into his windup and put everything he had into the pitch. The ball hit the burlap with so much force the fabric cracked loudly in the July air.

"Hey, hey boy!" the Greek yelled frantically.

Herman turned quickly to look.

The ragman splashed into the pond and pointed towards the center. "There's a girl in here, quick, fast as you can, to Rose! Get help!"

A girl? Herman thought.

Confused, he could only watch as the Greek plunged deeper into the pond.

And then a pair of hands, pale white and swollen with rot, came out of the water, and Herman gasped.

Someone is in the water!

He ran towards the pond and saw the ragman bend down to grasp the hands, and when he did, the Greek shrieked.

The sound pierced Herman's skull and caused him to stumble. He tripped on a small stone and fell into the grass. The ragman continued to scream as Herman struggled to his feet and caught sight of the man as he was dragged beneath the water.

The back door to the house opened up, and Rose raced out, followed by Herman's father. Movement in an upper window caught Herman's eye and he looked up.

Mr. Anderson stood in his library window, lit a cigar, and then he turned away.

Silence filled the air.

Rose and his father stood on the back steps, looks of horror on their faces as they looked at the pond. Other members of the staff joined them and the minutes ticked away.

Herman took a cautious step towards the pond.

"Herman, no!" his father yelled, and Herman stopped. As he looked to his father, the man shook his head. "No."

A moment later a curious 'pop' sounded, and the body of the ragman sprang to the surface of the pond. It floated face down, and Herman knew, without any doubt, the man was dead.

One of the gardeners came around the side of the house and called out to Herman's father, who nodded and descended the stairs. Together, the two men approached the pond. The body of the Greek drifted towards them as if guided by some unseen hand.

The two men stood patiently at the bank and waited. Herman gave the pond a wide berth and walked to them.

When he reached his father's side, he stole in close to the comfort of the large man's side. A heavy arm wrapped protectively around his shoulders, and together the three of them waited.

A few moments later, the body finally came to rest in the reeds.

"Hold tight, John," his father said as he let go of Herman.

"Alright, Barney," John said. When Herman's dad stepped towards the body, John moved forward. Herman watched as the gardener hooked his hands through the back of his father's braces and got a good grip. "Go ahead, Barney."

The man stepped down, one foot at a time, into the water. With each movement, he was poised to flee, and Herman had never seen his father act in such a way.

Finally, with a deep breath, he reached out, grabbed hold of the Greek's shirt and pulled.

John and Herman's father fell back onto the bank, the body of the Greek coming out of the water easily. It lay limply on the shore beside them.

"Damn him," John muttered. "Why doesn't he drain this God forsaken pond?"

"He likes to watch them die," Herman's father said, pushing himself into a sitting position. He looked down at the body and sighed. "He likes to watch them die."

Chapter 50: Walking towards her Room

"Who is she?" Marie asked.

"Hmm?" Herman said.

"The girl in the pond," Marie said. "Who is she?"

Shane looked back at Herman. "Did you ever find out?"

The older man was silent for a few minutes, and Shane thought he wasn't going to answer.

But then the man spoke.

"Yes," Herman said. "I did find out."

Both Shane and Marie kept silent and waited for him to elaborate.

Finally, Herman took a deep breath and said, "Her name is Vivienne Starr. I would like to tell you her wickedness came about from abuse. From some horrific incident in her life. Or, conversely, I would enjoy telling you she was a spoiled child who died terribly, and thus became the way she is.

"Neither, however, would be true," Herman said with a sigh. "She was always a wicked child, from what I have been able to learn. A foul wretch. One who pulled the wings off butterflies, not out of curiosity, but from a distinct desire to inflict pain."

"How long has she been here?" Marie asked.

"She and her family purchased the home which was built here in the early eighteen hundreds," Herman said. "They moved in during the summer of eighteen fifty-six."

The treetops shook, and Herman said, "Stop."

Shane did so.

The trees shook again.

"Telling stories, Herman?" a voice whispered from above. A woman's voice. "We taught you better."

The older man's face paled, and he swallowed nervously.

"What is it?" Marie asked in a low voice.

"My... my..." Herman's hand shook has he wiped the sweat off of his brow. "It is my mother's voice."

"Not only her voice," the woman said. "But all of her."

Shane caught a glimpse of something pale dart from one tree to another. He watched it and tried to get a closer look.

"It cannot be," Herman said, his voice growing stronger. "My mother was buried."

"This is not my flesh," the woman laughed, and Shane watched her drop down behind a tree. She peered around it, a pretty face framed by dark brown hair. With a wink at Shane, she disappeared back behind the tree. "I have no flesh. No body. Nothing."

"And why would my mother be here?" Herman asked.

"Who says I was ever allowed to leave?" his mother said, laughing. "And, what's more, why do you think you shall ever leave, my darling boy?"

"I will not be trapped here," he said defiantly. "She will not keep me here."

"Did you ever pitch to Danning, little man?" a man asked, and Shane watched as Herman stiffened. "I think not. The girl in the pond, yes, she saw to it. I think your fingers remember, yes?"

"The Greek," Herman whispered.

"Ah, Vasiliki Tripodis," the dead ragman chuckled. "Vasiliki Tripodis, and dead I am. Drowned by the girl. Should you be drowned, Herman, for bringing them here?"

"Yes," a deeper male voice said. "You've been ever so willful, my son."

"Is this real?" Marie asked in a low voice.

"I'm afraid it is," Herman said, his voice low and despondent.

Shane knew it as well. The old man's dead had come for him, and Shane wasn't sure if they would be able to stop the ghosts.

"Where are my parents?" Shane asked. He looked around and caught sight of bare flesh as the naked dead dashed from tree to tree. "Are they here too?"

The dead simply ignored them.

Instead, they continued to speak to Herman.

"Did you think you could come back and not suffer?" the man's mother asked. "Did you, Herman? You escaped once. She shall not let you away a second time. Oh no."

"And don't you wish to be with us, Herman?" his father asked. "We could be a family again. Who did they send you off to when the girl killed me? It was your mother's sister, was it not? It could only have been her. Unless they sent you to the Protestant orphanage, although I very much doubt they would have taken in a Jew."

"Come, Herman," Shane said, taking his eyes away from the forest. "We'll continue on."

"Damn it!" Marie yelled, and Shane turned in time to see a stocky, hairy man land on the path behind them. The man was naked, and he gave them all a lurid grin.

The Greek, Shane thought. He brought the bosun's whistle up to his lips, and as he blew a shrill note on it, Marie reached into her coat and pulled out a small automatic pistol.

She fired twice, the report of each shot loud and painful. Shane turned his head as he winced. His ears rang, and the stench of gunpowder filled his nose.

"Shane," Herman said.

Shane straightened up and looked around.

The forest was gone.

The three of them were in a narrow, dimly lit corridor. The roof was several feet up, and the walls were mere inches away on either side. Thick dust covered everything, and Shane had no idea where they were.

"Shane," Herman said again. "Look."

The older man pointed a crooked finger behind him, and Shane twisted around.

Half a dozen feet away a small door, painted white, marked the end of the hall. A brass doorknob, set into a plate made of the same metal, waited for one of them to turn it.

"Where does the door lead to?" Marie asked.

"It leads to her room," Herman said. "We will find Vivienne behind there if she is not busy in her pond."

Chapter 51: Shane, October 31st, 1990

The Halloween party was in full swing, and Shane had slipped away.

He knew what real ghosts were. What real monsters were. It still surprised him how his parents could be so nonchalant about it all at times, but then again, the dead didn't bother them.

Only him.

He didn't mind Eloise or Thaddeus. Carl was his friend. Even the old man, as frightful as he was, still had tried to help him. Roberto was always pleasant, on the rare occasion when Shane saw him.

But then there was the skeleton who had torn apart the parlor. The one who had caused his hair to fall off and never grow back.

The dark ones in the root cellar.

And the girl in the pond. The one who had possessed Mrs. Kensington.

The one who wanted him dead.

The one who had tried to drown his father.

Shane hated her.

He stood out in the backyard, by the pond. The lights of the house spilled out of the windows and cast long rectangles out over the grass.

Shane looked into the water and saw her. In the center of the pond, directly beneath the surface.

She waited.

She wanted him to get closer. To step up to the reed-lined bank where she could steal forward and snatch him into the water.

Part of him wanted to. Part of him wanted to fight her, to beat her. He felt he could, and part of him knew she feared him.

She must, Shane thought.

The water rippled, parted, and Vivienne rose up from the center. His stomach churned as her head appeared and nothing else.

Pale, wet blonde hair clung to her head, and Shane saw she wasn't more than thirteen or fourteen.

She glared at him.

"Come into the water, Shane," she said, her words skipping across the water like stones. "Come to me."

"Come out and see me," Shane said, clenching his hands into fists. "Would you like to go to the party?"

"An engagement?" she asked with a snicker. "Are you formally asking me to go with you, Shane?"

"Careful, my young friend," Carl said suddenly.

Shane didn't turn to look for the German, but he nodded.

"She seeks your death, of this I am certain."

"You're probably right," Shane said. *"I don't know if she can, though."*

"What are you saying?" she demanded. "I know you're talking to the German about me. Stop it!"

Carl said nothing more.

"Would you prefer I speak of you in English?" Shane asked.

"I would prefer you never spoke again," she snapped. She moved closer and her head cut the water like a bloated shark fin.

"You need to leave my house," she hissed. "Leave it or die."

"No," Shane said.

Vivienne grinned, and someone in the house screamed.

Not a playful scream, but one full of terror.

"You'll leave soon enough, Shane," she whispered and slipped back beneath her water.

He turned and sprinted for the house. In a moment, he was inside of the kitchen, and there was a man on the floor. Blood exploded out of his mouth as he vomited repeatedly and others were gathered around the man. They tried to help him as Shane's mother spoke frantically on the phone with someone.

"What happened?" Shane asked the person nearest to him, a woman he vaguely remembered having been introduced to.

"We don't know," she said in a shaky voice. "He was fine one minute, getting a beer out of the fridge, and then he just screamed and clutched his stomach. He's been throwing up blood."

The man collapsed onto his side, and someone caught him. The man looked at Shane, and his eyes went wide with fear.

"You!" the man gasped, and threw up again.

Shane staggered back as the man's bloody bile struck him in the face. The woman steadied him, and the man screamed again.

Shane watched the light flee from the man's eyes, and the Anderson House claimed another life.

Chapter 52: Going In

"Do we knock?" Marie asked, and Shane laughed in spite of the fear in the air.

Herman chuckled, the sound rife with anxiety, and said, "Yes. Shane, will you?"

Shane stepped forward, raised up his fist and knocked loudly several times.

No one answered.

He reached out, grabbed the doorknob and twisted. With a grunt, he pushed the door open.

A bright light burst out of the room, and Shane turned away. He blinked and rubbed at his eyes and finally was able to look in.

Dolls were piled haphazardly all over the furniture in the room. The bed and a rocker, a dresser and a side chair. Each of them was buried beneath dolls. Some of the dolls were ancient, nothing more than old cornhusk toys in rag clothing. Others were new as if taken fresh from a toy store shelf.

The room smelled sweetly of lilacs, and Shane remembered how much his mother hated the smell.

He took a few more steps into the room and Herman and Marie followed him. The detective walked to the left, the pistol still in her hand as she examined the dolls and the furniture.

"It has been a very long time," Herman said.

Shane looked at the man.

Herman smiled nervously. "A very long time since I was in this room. She has added to her collection."

"Why all the dolls?" Marie asked, finishing her circuit of the room.

"Trophies," Herman replied. "Mementos of those she has killed."

"Shane!"

Shane, Herman and Marie turned to the door.

Carl, flanked by Eloise and Thaddeus, stood in the doorway, just inside the hall.

"You must leave," Carl said, a note of desperation in his voice. *"She's coming. She's coming! She heard you in the forest. She knows you are here. You must flee, my friend!"*

Shane looked at Herman and Marie. "She's coming."

"What can we do?" Marie asked.

"Try to find my parents," Shane said, his voice suddenly raw. "Help me find my parents."

"We will," Herman said, nodding.

Shane turned to the dead. *"Thank you, my friend, but I must know where my parents are."*

Carl looked at Shane for a moment and then he said, *"We will hold her off for as long as we can."*

The door slammed closed.

Shane looked around the room.

"Herman," he said, "is there anywhere she might hide someone here?"

"The wardrobe," Herman said, gesturing towards a corner with his bent and crooked fingers.

"Wardrobe," Shane started to say, and then he stopped himself.

What he had assumed was molding for a window was in actuality the frame of a wardrobe built into the wall. Dolls were piled in front of it, and Marie stepped towards it. She put her weapon away and pulled down the dolls. Without a word she threw them onto the bed and Shane and Herman stayed out of her way.

Screams ripped through the room's closed door, and Shane jerked around.

The harsh sounds of a fight, vicious howls, and voices raised in anger, pushed their way through the wood.

A look back showed Marie as she cleared the last of the dolls.

The wardrobe's wide door opened of its own accord, and the noxious smell of old death bled into the room.

"Oh Jesus," Marie said, taking a stumbling step back.

"Shane," Herman said, reaching out a hand to steady him.

Shane shook his head as he stepped forward. The noise of the fight in the hall vanished, replaced by the thunderous beat of his own heart.

For all intents and purposes, the wardrobe's interior looked much as it should though it was barren of clothes. Shane's mother and father, however, hung from meat hooks set in the back of the piece of furniture.

They were dressed in their pajamas, their bodies thin husks, mummified. Between them stood a small marble plant stand. Upon the pale stone was a black house phone, similar to the one in the library.

The one through which he had spoken to his mother. If it had been her and not Vivienne.

"Shane," Marie said, "Shane we have to leave."

The words slowly pierced his sorrow. His rage grew, however, as he looked up at the bodies. Silence filled the hallway, and suddenly the door blew off the hinges.

Chapter 53: Vivienne Returns to Her Room

Shane turned slowly and faced the door.

Once more, he heard nothing except his heart. Vaguely he saw Marie rush past him and drop to the floor. Herman lay on his back, part of the door upon his small chest. Blood spilled from several cuts on his face.

He's hurt, Shane realized dully. Yet he could only remain focused on the doorway.

Focused on Vivienne.

She stood and grinned at him. Her long blonde hair was in a pair of ponytails, each tied with a bright blue ribbon. The blue matched her eyes.

She wore a white dress, the hem of which reached the floor while the sleeves ended at her wrists. On her hands, she wore a pair of brilliantly white gloves.

"Hello Shane," she said, stepping into the room.

"Vivienne," he said, his voice harsh.

She smiled. "You're upset?"

"Quite."

"Your parents?" she asked, feigning innocence.

"Yes."

She looked past him and into the wardrobe. "You know, they look remarkably well for being so dead."

From the corner of his eye, Shane saw Marie pull Herman farther from the doorway.

"They do," Shane agreed. "I was curious, though."

"Oh," Vivienne said, smiling sweetly, "about what?"

"Does your body look as well preserved?" he asked.

The smile vanished from her face. "Mine will look better than yours when I am finished with you, Shane Ryan."

"I doubt it," Shane replied.

Her nostrils flared as she took a step closer.

"I'm going to flay you alive," she whispered. "I've hated you for so long, Shane. Ever since you came here. Ever since you first slept in your room. I pushed them all to you, and yet you won them over. How?"

"I was never a spoiled brat," Shane answered. Her face went red, and he smiled. "Oh, you don't like names, do you?"

"I'll teach you," she spat. "I *will* teach you!"

Shane stood his ground as she lunged forward. She thrust her hands into his stomach and squeezed.

Nothing happened.

She looked up at him in surprise, a surprise which he was sure his own face mimicked.

"No!" She shrieked angrily. "No!"

She withdrew her hands, shoved them in again, and still nothing happened.

"The house is yours," a voice said in Italian. *"The dead have fought for you, and thus have made it yours."*

Roberto's violin began to play in the distance. A victorious march.

Shane reached out and put his hand on Vivienne's shoulder.

It was solid beneath his hand.

And everything about Vivienne flashed before him.

The wretched, vile girl; he saw her torture the hens and gut the cow. He watched her poison the serving girl and smother her infant brother. A burning image of her preparing to set the house on fire, the gleeful grin upon her face as she held up a flaming brand.

Her father, a great, tall, somber man. Miserable at what he had wrought with his own loins.

Shane saw her father come into the room and rip the torch from her small hand. Vivienne screamed at him in rage as her mother cowered in a corner, with a giant leather bound bible held up before her.

Vivienne laughed even as her father grabbed her by her shoulders, looked at her with a terrible inner pain, and picked her up.

The laughter and joy in her face vanished as he walked with fierce, stiff steps towards the pond.

Suddenly, she realized what he intended to do, and fought him. Great tufts of hair were ripped from his head. Blood sprang forth from a dozen cuts made by her nails. She sank her teeth into his back, yet he remained resolute.

He walked steadily down the bank, through the reeds and into the water. He tore her from his shoulders and thrust her into the pond.

The man wept as he drowned his daughter. Her white dress grew heavy and pulled her down as she thrashed. Fish scattered through the water, her eyes full of fear and rage as Vivienne tried to free herself. Her blonde hair slipped free of the ribbons to float like a halo about her pale face.

Shane shuddered and shook his head. He looked down at the beastly child in his hands.

Vivienne's mouth went slack with shock.

He tightened his grip, and she screamed.

Foul, dirty pond water burst from her lips and drenched his clothes.

"Marie," Shane said, looking over at the detective. "Get Herman to your uncle's."

Without a word she picked the small, old man up easily and hurried out of the room with him.

Vivienne tried to wrench herself free of Shane's grip, but she failed. She looked up into his face, and the wickedness which had filled her blue eyes vanished, replaced by terror.

"Where do you think you're going, young lady?" he whispered.

"Let me go," she hissed, trying to pull away again. "Let me go!"

Shane grabbed her other shoulder and squeezed. A sense of grim satisfaction slipped over him as she screamed. Her knees went weak, and only his tight grip kept her upright.

"Your parents are still here," she gasped. "Still here. Did you know?"

Shane kept the same amount of pressure on her, but he said, "I did not know, Vivienne. Why do you mention it?"

"Because I can free them, yes, yes I can. I can free them. They cannot leave the house, but they won't be trapped here. Not with me. I will let them go, if you will do the same," she said desperately, a whining tone in her voice.

"Will you?" Shane asked softly.

"Yes," she said, "just let me go, and I will free them."

162

Shane let go of one shoulder. "Free them first, Vivienne, and you shall follow."

"No," she said, grinning viciously. She screamed in pain as he tightened his grip with the other hand.

"Yes!" She shrieked. "Yes, fine!"

"Where are they?" Shane asked.

"In the bed tables drawer," she said. "Bring me there."

With his grip firmly on her shoulder, he half pushed, half dragged the dead girl over to the bed-table.

"Open it," he snapped.

Vivienne flinched, but she opened it as ordered.

A long, low moan escaped the drawer and something cold brushed past him.

He heard his parents weep as they fled the room.

"Freed," Vivienne said triumphantly. "Freed. And now for me, Shane Ryan."

"And what will you do? Where will you go?" he asked lightly.

She frowned, confused. "Why back to my pond, of course. I will keep my pond as I always have."

"So I thought," Shane whispered.

He looked at her for a long moment, until she finally demanded, "Let me go!"

Shane smiled. "I don't think so."

"You promised!" she screamed.

"No," Shane said, clenching his free hand into a fist and raising it above his head, "I never did."

He suddenly felt the power of the house, of all the bound dead flow through him. A deep, powerful energy surging inside of him. Beneath his hands, Vivienne was solid; a real form. An entity which could suffer and die; one which could be forced out of a world and into the next.

The power of the house, the energy of the dead who were loyal to him. All of it gave him a strength which no one, living or dead, could stand against.

As the spirits and the house surged inside of him, Shane discovered he could beat a ghost into oblivion.

Chapter 54: Two Weeks Later

"I spoke to Bernadette this morning," Marie said, taking a drink of her coffee.

"Herman is alright?" Shane asked, washing the last of the lunch dishes.

"Yes," she said. "The hospital will be releasing him in a few days. Uncle Gerry is still upset."

"About the whole 'adventure'?" Shane said, glancing over his shoulder at her.

"Of course," she said with a sigh.

"It's the Marine in him," he said, putting the last plate into the drying rack. He wiped his hands on the hand towel, hung it up to dry and went to the table.

"How are you feeling?" she asked.

He shrugged. "Partly in shock, I suppose."

"Have you had any luck getting back to her room, to recover your parents' bodies?"

"No," Shane said, rubbing the back of his head. "I haven't even been able to get to Roberto's room. No word from Carl, or Thaddeus or Eloise. Even the dark ones have been silent. I'm more afraid of the house now than I was when they were all raising a ruckus."

"Still drinking?" Marie asked.

"Yes," Shane answered. "The house may be quiet, Marie, but it doesn't mean my nightmares have gone away."

"Well, I'll say it again," she said as she stood up. "I'd be happy to sponsor you if you want to start the program, Shane."

"Thanks," Shane said. "I appreciate it."

"Listen, give me a call tomorrow. Maybe we can get coffee at some place other than your house or my uncle's," she said, grinning.

"Sounds good, Detective."

She chuckled. "I'll see myself out, Shane. Have a good day."

"You too, Marie," he said. He watched her leave the kitchen, waited for the front door to open and close, and then he walked to the pantry. Quickly he opened the door, lifted up the trap and descended into the root cellar.

He stood on the dirt floor and waited. Within a moment, the room darkened, and a voice said, "What do you want?"

"Answers," Shane snapped. His anger flared, and he fought back the urge to swear at the dark one.

"What answers do you think we have?" the dark one asked sulkily.

"Whatever ones I want," Shane answered angrily. "Have you found Carl and the others?"

"No."

"What of the old man?" Shane demanded.

"One of my brothers saw him in your parents' bathroom. And," the dark one hesitated.

"And what?" Shane asked.

"We saw your parents," it answered.

"Where?" Shane said excitedly.

"The library."

Shane turned around quickly and nearly slammed his head into the ladder. Hand over hand he quickly climbed up, flipped the trapdoor back into place and ran out the pantry. He took the stairs two at a time, grabbed hold of the banister and turned sharply towards the library.

The door, which he had closed earlier, was open.

The lights were on.

A fire burned in the hearth.

He stumbled over his own feet and nearly fell as he went into the room, and when he caught himself, he saw them.

Both his mother and his father.

Hank and Fiona Ryan.

Dead, but still they were there.

Each sat in a chair. Each held a book and a glass of wine.

They looked worn and battered, far older than he remembered, yet he knew it was from their time in hell with Vivienne.

His parents smiled at him.

Shane dropped to his knees and began to weep.

* * *

Bonus Scene Chapter 1: Meeting the Andersons

Carl sat patiently in the parlor of the Anderson house. His back was straight, his hands, palm down upon his thighs. It was always a comfort to slip into the habits the military had cultivated within him.

A coal fire burned in a brazier set within the confines of the large hearth. Beautiful club chairs of dark brown tooled leather were artfully arranged in the room. Each chair had its own table and tall floor lamps with sepia glass shades that stood as silent sentries behind each seat.

The large, dark wood door of the parlor opened with the faintest of whispers and the aged, respectful butler who had ushered him into the home stepped in.

"Herr Hesselschwerdt," the butler said, pronouncing Carl's surname effortlessly, "Mr. and Mrs. Anderson."

Carl stood up quickly and held himself rigid as the powerful couple entered the room.

They were in their late forties and impeccably dressed. Mr. Anderson could only be described as dashing, and his wife was stunning.

Mrs. Anderson's dark brown hair, streaked with single strands of silver, was piled elegantly on top of her head. Silver earrings graced her ears, and she was possibly the most beautiful woman Carl had ever had the pleasure of seeing in person. His breath caught in his throat, his heart hiccupped, and Carl forced himself to stay focused.

"Mr. Hesselschwerdt," Mr. Anderson said, offering his hand.

Carl stepped forward and shook it firmly. "Please, sir, call me Carl."

"A pleasure, Carl," Mr. Anderson said, releasing his hand. He turned partially and said, "This is my wife."

Carl gently accepted Mrs. Anderson's offered hand, bowed slightly over and let go. "A pleasure, madam."

Mrs. Anderson nodded her head, and Carl stepped back. Once the couple sat down, he returned to his own seat.

"Now, Carl," Mr. Anderson said, "could you please refresh my memory as to what your qualifications are for the job at hand?"

"Certainly, sir," Carl said. He focused his attention on Mr. Anderson rather than the beauty of Mrs. Anderson's hazel eyes. "You are seeking someone capable of interacting with the dead. I have the ability to do so. I can hear them, I can speak with them. I have worked for the Hancocks in Boston, the Rockefellers in New York, and the Kenyons in Providence. I have successfully communicated with the dead in their homes and succeeded in negotiating peace between the two sides."

"Peace?" Mrs. Anderson asked. The sound of her voice, delicate and musical, wrapped around him sensually.

"Yes madam," Carl said, hiding his reaction to her.

"You can't get rid of them?" Mr. Anderson asked with a frown.

"No sir," Carl said, shaking his head. "Most of them can be talked into leaving, but there are always some who will never quit a place. It is why I refuse to say I can free a home of the dead. Whether they stay or go, it is upon them. Some can be forced, but they can usually make their way back. And if that happens, it is never pleasant."

Mr. Anderson frowned. "This is not exactly what I wished to hear, Carl."

"I am sorry, sir," Carl said, his hopes crashing. "I will not lie, though."

Mr. Anderson's frown slowly changed into a smile, and he nodded. "I would rather it be so. You think you can, what is it, negotiate a treaty of some sort with them?"

"I can only do my best, sir," Carl said. "And I do not accept payment until a job is complete."

"I can respect such a policy," Mr. Anderson said, "but it is unnecessary for us. We are comfortable, in regards to personal funds, so I will pay you up front. You need to live, sir. When can you start?"

"Tomorrow morning," Carl said, barely able to contain his excitement. "Tomorrow morning I will begin if the time is good for you."

"It is," Mr. Anderson said. "Just be prepared, Carl. Be prepared."

Bonus Scene Chapter 2: In the Kitchen

Carl sat at the servant's table at the back of the large kitchen. A steaming cup of strong black coffee sat in front of him as did his notebook and pencil.

The giant grandfather clock in the center hallway struck the hour.

Six AM, Carl thought. Sunlight filtered in through the windows over the sink and highlighted the metalwork on the large stove which occupied a great portion of the left wall. The housekeeper stood across the table from him, a tall, beautiful woman in her early fifties.

Elizabeth, Carl reminded himself. *Elizabeth Grady.*

She looked as though she brokered no-nonsense amongst the staff, and she reminded him of some of the sergeants he had served under. She was, Carl felt certain, extremely competent and respected.

"Mrs. Grady," Carl said, smiling. "Would you do me the honor of sitting down?"

A flicker of a smile passed her lips, and she nodded her head slightly.

Carl stood up, waited for her to sit, and then he resumed his seat.

"May I ask how long you have been employed by the Andersons?" Carl asked.

"Yes, of course," she said, her voice carrying only the slightest hint of an Irish accent. "I have been a member of the Anderson staff since Mrs. Anderson married Mr. Anderson twenty-two years ago. Before that, I was Mrs. Anderson's maid."

"When did the Anderson's move into the house?" Carl asked.

"Nineteen thirty-two," she replied.

Carl glanced around. "Do you know how old the house is?"

She shook her head. "No, but her bones are old. Long before the war of the rebellion, though not as old as the revolution."

Carl jotted the information down, looked up at her and said, "Mrs. Grady, you do not strike me as a woman given to flights of fancy."

"Indeed, I am not, sir," she said proudly.

"I will believe you, regardless of how bizarre or queer the story might sound to you in your retelling," Carl said gently. "So please, do not hesitate to tell me everything."

"Well, sir," she said, her face tight, "I must say what I have experienced is disturbing. I've children of my own, and I know the sounds they make. Do you understand?"

Carl nodded.

"Good." she leaned forward and whispered, "There are dead children here, sir. Two at least, perhaps more."

"Do you know their names?" he asked.

"Yes," she said, fidgeting nervously for the first time. "A little girl, named Eloise. A little boy named Thaddeus. They are not wicked, sir, and I would not see you drive them out."

"It is not my intention to drive them out of the house," Carl said reassuringly. "I seek only to establish peace between the living and the dead."

"Well then," Mrs. Grady said, "it is not the children to whom you should speak."

"Who then?"

"Whatever lurks within the root cellar," Mrs. Grady said, casting a fearful glance at the pantry door. "I don't let my girls go down into the cellar unless they're in pairs, and unless a third is at the ladder with a lantern."

The fear emanating from the woman was palpable.

"Have you gone in the root cellar?" Carl asked.

"Yes," she whispered. "I try to go myself, if something is needed, and I bring Mary with me. She's the strongest. Occasionally though I am busy, and one of the others accompanies her. But not the cooks."

"No?" Carl said.

Mrs. Grady shook her head in disgust. "They're afraid, the cowardly things. Too afraid. Especially after what happened to Emily."

"What happened to Emily?" Carl asked.

"The things in the root cellar did," Mrs. Grady said, leaning back in her chair. "You see, Emily would stand in the pantry and mock the girls for their fear. She would mock the things in the root cellar, saying they've no power in the light of Christ. I told her, as good a Catholic as I try to be, even I know there are things which the Good Lord does not rein in. And some of those things are in the root cellar."

"Did she continue to mock them?" Carl said.

Mrs. Grady nodded.

"What happened?"

"They took her sight," Mrs. Grady said, glancing once more at the closed pantry door. "They pulled her down the ladder when she went into the pantry for beans. Dragged her down screaming. When we pulled her up, her eyes were milky white, and she couldn't see a thing."

Carl wrote the information down. When he finished, he said, "Mrs. Grady, have any others been harmed by the things in the root cellar?"

"No," she said, shaking her head. "But we lost a gardener, and I think he went down there."

"Why would the gardener go into the root cellar?" Carl said, confused.

"On a dare," Mrs. Grady said sadly. "Before she went blind, Emily dared him to go down. As he did, though, she was called out to the back for a delivery from the grocer. When she came back, the gardener was gone. None saw him again, although Emily said the door to it had been open when she came back in with the goods. Since he didn't answer when she called out, she closed it tight."

Carl added the story to his notes. After a moment, he looked at Mrs. Grady and asked, "Mrs. Grady, has anyone else had any experiences in the root cellar, other than Emily?"

"Yes," she said. "Mary, the girl who helps me the most. She's been down more times than me, and her hair has gone white because of it."

"Do you think you might send her in next?" Carl asked.

"Of course, sir," she answered.

"Thank you," Carl said, "you have been extremely helpful, Mrs. Grady."

She rose up and nodded. She paused and then she asked hurriedly, "And you won't chase the children out?"

"No," Carl said seriously. "It would not cross my mind to do so."

"Very good, sir," she said, relieved. "I will send Mary in to you."

"Thank you," Carl said. He sat back down, looked over the notes quickly, and then wrote the name 'Mary' on a fresh page.

A few minutes passed, and Mary came in. Her pale face was flushed as though she had hurried to him. Her hair, from what he could see beneath her hat, was bright white. Her eyes were brown, and her face was spotted with freckles. She was shorter and stouter than Mrs. Grady, but she was a pretty young woman with a look of intelligence.

Carl stood up and smiled warmly. "Please, Mary, sit down."

Mary did so and smiled nervously. "Are you German, sir?"

"I am," Carl said cautiously, sitting down. "Does it bother you?"

"No," she said. "It's just my brother always referred to Germans as beasts and, well."

"You thought perhaps I might be hairy with great big teeth?" he asked, smiling.

She blushed as she nodded.

"It is alright," Carl said. "I was told the Irish couldn't function without whiskey. Each government likes to speak ill of others. Especially during war."

"Yes sir," Mary said.

"I am not offended, though," Carl added quickly. "I am not offended at all."

"Thank you, sir," she said, relieved.

"Now," he said, taking up his pencil, "what can you tell me about the root cellar?"

Bonus Scene Chapter 3: In the Butler's Pantry

Carl stood in the butler's pantry and looked down at the closed wooden trapdoor set in the center of the floor. A small brass ring, neatly set within a matching groove, offered the only way to open it.

Something scratched behind the pantry's shelves.

"Hello," Carl said.

No one answered.

Carl turned around, nodded to Mrs. Grady, who stood by the stove with the chef Joan, and closed the door. A single electric bulb lit the space.

"Hello," he said again, in a lower voice.

"Hello," a young girl finally said from the darkness of a far corner.

"Are you Eloise?" Carl asked.

"I am," she said. "Why are you here?"

"To talk with you, and with Thaddeus," Carl said honestly. "And, to speak with those in the root cellar."

Eloise was silent.

He waited several minutes before he called out her name again.

"Yes," she answered.

"Who is in the root cellar?"

"The dark ones," she whispered. "Her's. You don't want to go in there. Stay up here and talk with me. Talk with Thaddeus. Talk with all of us."

"There are more of you?" he asked.

"Of course," she said with a giggle. The giggle faded, and she said, "But don't go into the root cellar. They won't like you. She won't like it."

"Who is she?" he said.

"No," Eloise said petulantly. "I don't want to talk about her. She doesn't like it."

"Well," Carl said, "does she live in the house, too?"

"No. But she decides what happens."

"Ah," Carl said. "I do need to go down and to speak with them, though."

"They may kill you," Eloise said. "They don't like people. They don't like anyone."

"Do you know who they are?" Carl asked.

"No," she whispered. "But I know when they came."

"When?" Carl asked softly. "When did they come here, Eloise?"

"When the Andersons came," she said, her voice barely audible. "When the Andersons came, and Mr. Anderson put the books into the library. They came then, and they will not leave. The old man hates them. Thaddeus and I are... we're afraid of them. And she, she loves them."

"Thank you, Eloise," Carl said. He looked at the trapdoor. He took off his jacket, folded it neatly and put it beside a basket of apples on a middle shelf. He carefully removed his cufflinks, placed them on top of the jacket, and then rolled his sleeves. His scars, a physical reminder of his wartime injuries, seemed to dance across his flesh.

He smiled at them, grabbed hold of the brass ring, and pulled the trapdoor open.

Carl took a deep breath to calm himself, and then descended the ladder into pure darkness.

Bonus Scene Chapter 4: A Conversation

The air was cold and stank of death, a smell Carl remembered vividly from the woods of France.

He closed the door to the root cellar behind him. He climbed down the rest of the way, found the dirt floor with his feet, and stood alone in the darkness.

Things moved around him.

Small things.

"Are you here?" Carl asked in a low voice.

The things stopped.

"Will you speak with me?"

Something scrambled up his leg, pierced his flesh with a sharp, cold sensation and then slipped away.

Carl bit back a scream.

An icy tongue dragged across his cheek, teeth nipped at his ears, and a hand wrapped itself in his hair.

Carl let his head be pulled back, his throat exposed.

Fingernails dragged across it and paused to grip his larynx tightly before letting go.

Suddenly, the teeth vanished from his ears and the hand slipped out of his hair.

"What do you want?" a deep and powerful male voice asked.

"I seek a truce," Carl said.

"A truce?" a second voice asked.

"We have no quarrel with you," the first voice said. "You bared your neck."

"Accepted your fate," said a third voice.

"You have faced death," the second voice finished.

"Many times," Carl agreed. "I am not here for myself, however. I come on behalf of the people who live in the house."

"Who?" the first voice demanded. "For whom do you speak?"

"For all," Carl answered.

"Who called upon you for this task?" the second asked, snarling.

"Mr. Anderson," Carl said, and the voices howled. The earth shuddered beneath his feet and jars rattled on the shelves. Someone cried out nervously above him.

"Did he?" the third voice asked, hissing. "Did he now?"

"We are here because of him," the second voice snapped.

"He bound us and brought us," the first said angrily. "Brought us here, sought to keep us, but he did not know about her. No, not at all."

"She freed us," the second said.

"She gave us this place," the third finished. "Gave it to us. The root cellar is ours, to do with as we please."

"Some nights," the second said, the voice suddenly soft and close to Carl. "Yes, some nights and some days even, stranger, we are allowed out. We slip through the walls of the house, and we *torment* him."

"Remind him," the first said with a sigh. "We remind him of what he's done."

"We shall make no truce. None yet," the third said. "Not until we have had our way with Anderson and have helped to reap what he has sown."

"What has he sown?" Carl asked. "What has he done?"

"Ask him," the first voice said, laughing bitterly. "Ask him. Beware, though, there are far worse things than us in this house. And not all of them dead, either."

The trapdoor flew open, and the bright light of the butler's pantry flooded the root cellar and momentarily blinded him.

Carl grimaced, closed his eyes tightly against the light and waited a moment for his vision to adjust.

When he opened his eyes again, he looked around.

While the root cellar still stank of death, Carl knew he was alone with the food.

The dark ones had slipped away.

They had told him, however, what he needed in order to prepare a truce.

Carl turned and climbed the ladder.

Bonus Scene Chapter 5: Once More in the Parlor

Carl got to his feet as Mrs. Anderson walked into the room.

He gave a polite bow and waited for her to sit. As he sat down, he said politely, "Madam, I am sorry. I had thought they had informed Mr. Anderson of the request."

"My husband is away on business in Boston, I am afraid," she said, smiling at him. "I hope I may be of some service to you."

"Perhaps you will be," Carl said, excited at being in her presence. She smelled of lilacs, and the scent teased his nose.

"Before we begin," she said, placing her hands on her lap, "I must ask, have you had any luck? I know you have questioned my domestics thoroughly."

"I have had a bit of luck," Carl answered. "Mrs. Grady and Mary were quite helpful."

"Mrs. Grady is my rock," Mrs. Anderson said, smiling. "She has been since I was a girl. Tell me, though, what have you accomplished?"

"I have spoken with some of the dead," Carl said, and Mrs. Anderson's eyes widened.

"Truthfully?" she asked.

He nodded.

"What did they say?"

"Well, two of them told me it was not they who were the ones causing the trouble at night. It was a group of others. Some who have sheltered in the root cellar."

Mrs. Anderson stiffened slightly. "The root cellar."

"Yes," Carl said. "Have you heard of troubles there?"

"Whispers," she said softly. "From a dead girl who creeps into my rooms at night."

Carl frowned and got to his feet. He paced back and forth for a moment, turned and looked at Mrs. Anderson as he asked, "Madam, was this Eloise?"

Mrs. Anderson's eyes widened, and she nodded.

"Well, she has told you the truth," Carl said. He went to return to his seat, and he paused. For the first time, he noticed a tall cabinet, filled with scores of photographs; postcards of soldiers from the Great War. Americans, British, French, and even Germans.

He turned and looked at her. "Mrs. Anderson, where did you get these photographs?"

She looked at the cabinet and smiled sadly. "I buy them when I find them."

She stood up and with immeasurable grace came to stand beside him. Carl felt drunk by her presence.

"Shortly after the end of the war, I found the picture on the bottom left there," she said, pointing at a stained and tattered photograph. "It was in the street. No name upon it. The photographer had died and his studio was closed. I tried to see if anyone knew the soldier by having an advertisement run in the paper, but no one responded. I could not bear the thought of him not being remembered. Shortly after, I found the one of the young man in the German uniform. And so it continued."

Carl looked at the photographs and wondered if he had killed any of them. The chance was slim, of course, but there was always the chance.

Always.

"Yes," he said softly after a minute. "There were many who were forgotten."

"Did you fight?" Mrs. Anderson asked looking at him.

"I did," Carl said, turning away from the pictures. "In fact, I have a photograph of myself. I carry it with me."

Mrs. Anderson raised an eyebrow at the statement and Carl chuckled.

"It is not conceit, Mrs. Anderson, nor narcissism." Carl reached into his coat and removed his billfold. He opened the old, soft leather case and took out the trimmed photographic postcard of himself. He handed it to Mrs. Anderson.

She accepted it gracefully and smiled at the photo as she looked at it. "You look barely old enough to shave here, Carl."

Carl smiled and nodded. "Yes. I look exceptionally young in uniform. Many times I was forced to provide proof of my age. Well, at the beginning of the war at least."

She turned the card over and frowned as she tried to make sense of the Gothic German script on the back.

"What does it say?" she asked after a moment, looking up at Carl.

Carl closed his eyes and recited the words from memory. "My dearest little boy, here is the photograph which you had taken for me. I had the photographer produce several since I know Ada would want one as well. Write to me soon, my little boy, and let your worrying mother know you are well. Love always, your mother."

Carl opened his eyes and smiled at Mrs. Anderson. "My mother died in a fire when I was a prisoner of the Americans at the end of the war. The photograph is the only physical item I have of both my mother and my home."

"I'm sorry to hear of your mother's death," Mrs. Anderson said softly, a sad smile on her face. She started to say something more, but a scream ripped through the air.

Carl stuffed his billfold back into his coat as he ran for the door.

The butler nearly struck him as he opened it, the man's face white with terror.

"Herr Hesselschwerdt," the butler said. "Upstairs!"

Carl nodded and raced past the man to the long stairs. He raced up and found a maid on the floor. She was flanked on either side by other domestics and Mrs. Grady stood pale faced above them.

"Mrs. Grady," Carl said, panting as he came to a stop. "What happened?"

"The passage," the woman said grimly. She pointed to a bedroom.

Carl quickly went into the room and saw an open door, a slim secretive passage through which the servants came and went.

Carl stepped in and felt the cold air. He watched as the lights flickered.

He was not alone in the passage.

Something small and dark raced by.

The dark ones.

More dashed along the edges as the lights went out.

Carl beat back his fear and asked in a calm voice, "Why are you out of the cellar?"

The first voice he had heard below the butler's pantry spoke.

"She let us out," the voice answered. "She has let us run free today. Anderson is busy in his library. And no truce, none while he still lives."

"Anderson is in Boston," Carl said, yet even as he spoke he wondered if it were true.

"Really?" the voice sneered. "Knock on the door and see if the man is there. No peace for him. No peace."

"And the maid? Why attack her?" Carl asked, anger now threatening to spill into his words.

"We blessed her. We saved her. And though struck and unconscious, she is alive," the voice chuckled. "Although barren. We've robbed her of it. She'll thank us, should she survive Anderson's *attentions*."

The lights burst back into life and warmth flooded the passage.

I must speak with Anderson, Carl thought angrily. *I must know what is going on.*

Bonus Scene Chapter 6: In the Library

Mrs. Grady looked up at Carl as he stepped into the hall.

"Mrs. Grady," Carl said as calmly as he could. "Which room is the library?"

"There, sir," she said, turning slightly to point at a closed door. "Why?"

"I must speak with Mr. Anderson," Carl answered, starting towards the room. The butler hurried to intercept him.

"Mr. Anderson is away on business in Boston today, sir," the man said.

"Then he will not mind me going into the library," Carl said determinedly. "I do believe I am granted free rein to investigate the house in order to purge it of the dead."

The butler straightened up. "The library, sir, is off limits."

Carl stopped and looked at the man. After a moment, he said, "Do you see the girl on the floor behind me?"

The butler kept his eyes on Carl and nodded.

"And I do believe there was a cook robbed of her sight?"

While the man's face remained impassive his Adam's apple bobbed once with a nervous swallow. "There was."

"Death awaits in the root cellar," Carl continued. "The girl behind me, they said what they did to her was a kindness. Will you throw away all of your lives? I must enter the library."

"Thomas," Mrs. Grady said softly, "I do believe someone is at the main door."

The butler's eyes met Mrs. Grady's and a moment later he nodded. Without a word, he stepped out of Carl's way and descended the stairs.

Carl walked to the library door, opened it, quickly stepped inside and closed it behind him.

The room was dim. The single green-shaded light on the desk was weak and barely illuminated Mr. Anderson, who sat in a tall chair and looked at Carl in surprise.

On the desk, a large swath of purple velvet covered the blotter. Upon the cloth lay a dozen sets of teeth. Teeth still bound in their human jaws. A bottle of bourbon stood just to the left of the cloth, and a half empty glass of the same was beside it.

Mr. Anderson leaned back, and a curious smile crossed his face.

"Carl," the man said. "To what do I owe this surprise?"

"I've come to speak with you about the dead," Carl said.

"Really?" Mr. Anderson asked, chuckling. He pushed himself away from the desk and stood up. "You've negotiated a truce already with them, have you?"

"Of course not," Carl snapped, keeping his eyes on Mr. Anderson as the man walked to a bookshelf and fidgeted with a book.

"Then why bother me?" Mr. Anderson asked, turning his back to Carl.

"I need to know what it is you have done to the dead in the root cellar," Carl said, glancing at the sets of teeth on the desk. "Why do they hate you?"

He turned and faced Carl, a large revolver in his hand. "For the same reason you're going to hate me," Mr. Anderson said.

Carl looked at the weapon and smiled. "Mr. Anderson, I am not afraid of death. I'm sure you know this."

"Oh, I do," Mr. Anderson said, laughing. "I do. I'm not going to kill you. At least not immediately. But I'll hurt you, enough so you won't be able to interrupt me. A stomach wound perhaps. Then, I'll hurt my dear wife in front of you."

Carl's breath caught in his throat.

Mr. Anderson grinned. "Yes. My wife. I've noticed she's taken quite a liking to you. Quite a liking indeed. Were we not married and you and I were chasing her hand, well, I do believe you might come out on top. However, such a thing is neither here nor there, now is it?"

Carl shook his head.

"Now, I won't be taking your teeth, or doing anything else I did with the others," Mr. Anderson said, the playful tone in his voice vanishing. "No. I won't do any of those things. I don't particularly want you hanging around in the root cellar.

"Those gentlemen," Mr. Anderson said, gesturing towards the teeth with his free hand, "I like having them where they are. Trapped. True, they make life a little bothersome at times, but they're a pleasant reminder of the men I've beaten in business. I've been collecting their teeth since I was thirteen, Carl. Thirteen. I've been killing longer than you've been born."

"You enjoy it," Carl said, warily watching the man.

"Yes," Mr. Anderson said sincerely. "I enjoy it tremendously. You see, to be quite honest with you, Herr Hesselschwerdt, I believed you to be a complete and utter charlatan.

"I only brought you in," he continued, "in an effort to get the help to stop their complaining, you see. You were to be my snake oil, a little bit of eyewash to make everything look alright. A bit of that proverbial 'balm of Gilead,' if you will. I simply wanted them all to stop their ceaseless prattling."

Mr. Anderson sighed and shook his head. "Your real abilities have been more of a hindrance than of a help. As I'm sure you can imagine."

"Well," Carl said, "what will you do with me?"

"I will forget you," Mr. Anderson said, his voice suddenly hard and brutal. He kept the barrel of the pistol leveled on Carl as he stepped to a bookcase, reached in with his free hand and pressed a small latch.

A large click sounded, and Mr. Anderson sidestepped to the right. He pulled the bookcase out and revealed a door behind it. Without even looking, he grasped the door's handle and pushed it to the left. The thing slid on silent tracks and revealed a smooth wall of either stone or concrete.

"Come here," Mr. Anderson said, stepping away.

Carl hesitated.

"Stand in front of the doorway and then turn around and face me."

Carl's mind raced as he did so. He could think of nothing, though, for every thought returned to images of Mrs. Anderson being tortured at the hands of her husband. Of being forced to watch her physical destruction.

He knew the man could do it. He had no doubt.

Carl stepped towards him and reached the doorway. He saw a hole in the floor in front of him and then he turned around to face Anderson.

As he did so, the man lunged forward, caught Carl off balance and knocked him backward.

Carl stumbled, tripped and suddenly felt nothing beneath his feet.

He fell, for a long, terrible moment, and when he struck the bottom of the hole, his legs broke. Carl screamed in agony as the pain instantly flooded him. His head pounded as he twisted to look up. Far above him, he could see a pale, round light which marked the entrance to the hole he was in.

Mr. Anderson leaned over, reached for a light switch and turned it on.

Carl winced and closed his eyes as the bright light poured out of bulbs set in the walls.

"Ah," Mr. Anderson said cheerfully, "you survived the fall. I'm quite glad. Quite glad. You'll provide me with a bit of entertainment, and, I must confess, I don't get nearly enough of it."

Once more, the joyful tone vanished, and Mr. Anderson continued to speak. "Eventually, though, Carl, I will forget about you. The world will forget about you. This is my oubliette. My little place of forgetting. I shall forget you."

Mr. Anderson reached in, turned off the light, and disappeared.

Carl heard the door start to close, and he was plunged into darkness.

He lay on the hard stone floor, and a chill stole over him. The pain was terrible, fear started to eat at him, and suddenly he laughed.

She has my photograph, he thought, resting his head on the stone. *She has my photograph. She will remember.*

She won't forget me.

Carl's laughter broke into sobs, as he wept upon the cold stone floor.

* * *

<u>FREE Bonus Novel!</u>

Wow, I hope you enjoyed this book as much as I did writing it! If you enjoyed the book, please leave a review. Your reviews inspire me to continue writing about the world of spooky and untold horrors!

To really show you my appreciation for purchasing this book, please enjoy a **FREE extra spooky bonus novel.** This will surely leave you running scared!

Visit below to download your bonus novel and to learn about my upcoming releases, future discounts and giveaways: www.ScareStreet.com

<u>FREE books (30 - 60 pages):</u>
<u>Ron Ripley (Ghost Stories)</u>
1. Ghost Stories (Short Story Collection)
   www.scarestreet.com/ghost

<u>A.I. Nasser (Supernatural Suspense)</u>
2. Polly's Haven (Short Story)
   www.scarestreet.com/pollys
3. This is Gonna Hurt (Short Story)
   www.scarestreet.com/thisisgonna

<u>Multi-Author Scare Street Collaboration</u>
4. Horror Stories: A Short Story Collection
   www.scarestreet.com/horror

<u>And experience the full-length novels (150 – 210 pages):</u>
<u>Ron Ripley (Ghost Stories)</u>
1. Sherman's Library Trilogy (FREE via mailing list signup)
   www.scarestreet.com
2. The Boylan House Trilogy
   www.scarestreet.com/boylantri
3. The Blood Contract Trilogy
   www.scarestreet.com/bloodtri

4. The Enfield Horror Trilogy
   www.scarestreet.com/enfieldtri

Moving In Series

5. **Moving In Series Box Set Books 1 - 3 (22% off)**
   www.scarestreet.com/movinginbox123
6. Moving In (Book 1)
   www.scarestreet.com/movingin
7. The Dunewalkers (Moving In Series Book 2)
   www.scarestreet.com/dunewalkers
8. Middlebury Sanitarium (Book 3)
   www.scarestreet.com/middlebury
9. **Moving In Series Box Set Books 4 - 6 (25% off)**
   www.scarestreet.com/movinginbox456
10. The First Church (Book 4)
    www.scarestreet.com/firstchurch
11. The Paupers' Crypt (Book 5)
    www.scarestreet.com/paupers
12. The Academy (Book 6)
    www.scarestreet.com/academy

Berkley Street Series

13. Berkley Street (Book 1)
    www.scarestreet.com/berkley
14. The Lighthouse (Book 2)
    www.scarestreet.com/lighthouse
15. The Town of Griswold (Book 3)
    www.scarestreet.com/griswold
16. Sanford Hospital (Book 4)
    www.scarestreet.com/sanford
17. Kurkow Prison (Book 5)
    www.scarestreet.com/kurkow
18. Lake Nutaq (Book 6)
    www.scarestreet.com/nutaq
19. Slater Mill (Book 7)
    www.scarestreet.com/slater
20. Borgin Keep (Book 8)
    www.scarestreet.com/borgin
21. Amherst Burial Ground (Book 9)
    www.scarestreet.com/amherst

Hungry Ghosts Street Series

David Longhorn (Supernatural Suspense)
The Sentinels Series
37. Sentinels (Book 1)
www.scarestreet.com/sentinels
38. The Haunter (Book 2)
www.scarestreet.com/haunter
39. The Smog (Book 3)
www.scarestreet.com/smog
Dark Isle Series
40. Dark Isle (Book 1)
www.scarestreet.com/darkisle
41. White Tower (Book 2)
www.scarestreet.com/whitetower
42. The Red Chapel (Book 3)
www.scarestreet.com/redchapel
Ouroboros Series
43. The Sign of Ouroboros (Book 1)
www.scarestreet.com/ouroboros
44. Fortress of Ghosts (Book 2)
www.scarestreet.com/fortress
45. Day of The Serpent (Book 3)
www.scarestreet.com/serpent
Curse of Weyrmouth Series
46. Curse of Weyrmouth (Book 1)
www.scarestreet.com/weyrmouth
47. Blood of Angels (Book 2)
www.scarestreet.com/bloodofangels

Eric Whittle (Psychological Horror)
Catharsis Series
48. Catharsis (Book 1)
www.scarestreet.com/catharsis
49. Mania (Book 2)
www.scarestreet.com/mania
50. Coffer (Book 3)
www.scarestreet.com/coffer
Sara Clancy (Supernatural Suspense)
Dark Legacy Series

51. Black Bayou (Book 1)
   www.scarestreet.com/bayou
52. Haunted Waterways (Book 2)
   www.scarestreet.com/waterways
53. Demon's Tide (Book 3)
   www.scarestreet.com/demonstide

Banshee Series
54. Midnight Screams (Book 1)
   www.scarestreet.com/midnight
55. Whispering Graves (Book 2)
   www.scarestreet.com/whispering
56. Shattered Dreams (Book 3)
   www.scarestreet.com/shattered

Black Eyed Children Series
57. Black Eyed Children (Book 1)
   www.scarestreet.com/blackeyed
58. Devil's Rise (Book 2)
   www.scarestreet.com/rise
59. The Third Knock (Book 3)
   www.scarestreet.com/thirdknock

Demonic Games Series
60. Demonic Games (Book 1)
   www.scarestreet.com/nesting
61. Buried (Book 2)
   www.scarestreet.com/buried

Chelsey Dagner (Supernatural Suspense)
Ghost Mirror Series
62. Ghost Mirror (Book 1)
   www.scarestreet.com/ghostmirror
63. The Gatekeeper (Book 2)
   www.scarestreet.com/gatekeeper

Keeping it spooky,
Team Scare Street

CPSIA information can be obtained
at www.ICGtesting.com
Printed in the USA
LVHW041503270919
632501LV00010B/501/P

9 781532 759208